THE HOUSEKEEPER'S BILLIONAIRE BOSS

A CAPROCK CANYON ROMANCE BOOK THREE

BREE LIVINGSTON

Edited by
CHRISTINA SCHRUNK

The Housekeeper's Billionaire Boss

Copyright © 2019 by **Bree Livingston**

Edited by Christina Schrunk

https://www.facebook.com/christinaschrunk.editor

Proofread by Krista R. Burdine

https://www.facebook.com/iamgrammaresque

Cover design by Victorine Lieske

http://victorinelieske.com/

All rights reserved. No part of this publication may be reproduced, distributed or transmitted in any form or by any means, without prior written permission.

Bree Livingston

https://www.breelivingston.com

Publisher's Note: This is a work of fiction. Names, characters, places, and incidents are a product of the author's imagination. Locales and public names are sometimes used for atmospheric purposes. Any resemblance to actual people, living or dead, or to businesses, companies, events, institutions, or locales is completely coincidental.

The Housekeeper's Billionaire Boss/ Bree Livingston. -- 1st ed.

ISBN: 9781701594159

This is dedicated to my husband:

Twenty-one years.
Two kids.
Four cats.
And a lot of fun.

I don't say it often enough, but you are one of the best things to ever happen to me. I'm not sure how you put up with me sometimes. Thank you for loving me. Loving our girls. Supporting me. Being a Godly example for me and my girls. Thank you for being loving and kind and wonderful. You're the caramel in my popcorn.

PROLOGUE

Rushing from one machine to the other, Molly Hines didn't possess enough arms to tackle a coffee shop short-staffed on a Monday. Only two weeks on the job, and she didn't know enough to handle a rush. She certainly didn't have all of the drinks memorized yet. Then the special orders on top of that? Her brain was mush by the time she went home each day.

A large man reached the counter, and she took his order, but not before seeing the cute guy who'd been coming in since she'd started working there. Her heart fluttered in her chest, and her face flushed. Josiah, the only thing she knew about him so far. Well, other than he always dressed professionally with a nice button-up and slacks under a long tweed coat. Dapper. That was the best word for him.

After she took the huge guy's order, Josiah stepped up to the counter. Oh, he was gorgeous with his thick dark hair and a curl in the middle of his forehead, like Clark Kent, that he continually pushed back.

"Hey," she said and tucked a piece of hair behind her ear.

Of course, she didn't need to be acting like that. She had a boyfriend, and she wasn't that kind of girl. They hadn't been dating super long, but they were serious enough to be talking about long-term stuff. Clearly, her head and her heart needed a meeting of the minds to get on the same page about her current relationship. The cute guy was totally out of her league anyway.

"What would you like today?" she said and tried to not seem like a complete flake. She knew the answer, but she didn't want him to think she was a stalker or something. Who memorizes a complete stranger's drink choices?

"Uh, could I get a caramel macchiato?"

"Sure," she replied.

She finished ringing him up and slapped the printed ticket on a cup. He drifted over to the corner as the next customer began rattling off a drink order.

Just as the next ticket printed, her manager barged over, holding a cup with steam pouring from it. "Another drink made incorrectly. This is the third one today." He did nothing to keep his voice down, and now everyone was looking at her.

"Uh," she stammered. "I'm sorry. I'm trying."

"Not hard enough. Look, it's coffee, sweetheart, not rocket science. You take the order, fix the drink using the directions, and that's it." His voice only seemed to get louder. "What's so difficult about that?"

"I—"

"You're fired. Leave the apron on your way out."

Molly's lip trembled and tears threatened. No way was she letting this jerk see her cry. She quickly untied the apron and threw it at him, grabbed her purse sitting on a shelf below the register, and stomped out.

She got half a block before reaching a nearby restaurant that had outdoor seating and dropped into a wire-backed chair. Then the tears flowed. Stupid, stupid crying. She hated it.

"Uh, Molly?"

She jerked her head up at the sound of her name. Josiah had followed her? "Yeah," she said, realizing she probably looked like a drowned cat. She furiously wiped at her eyes. "How do you know my name?"

He tapped his chest as he smiled. "Name tag."

Great. Her cheeks burned with embarrassment, and she grimaced. "Right."

"Mind if I sit?" he asked.

Shaking her head, she waved at the chair next to hers. "No." She sniffed and realized he didn't have a drink in his hand. "You didn't even get your macchiato?"

He shook his head, pushing that curl back. "No, and I won't be going back either. That guy was a jerk. You don't treat people like that."

"I never should have taken the job. He was a jerk from the beginning." Tears pooled in her eyes again. He'd made her feel stupid.

"Uh, I hope this doesn't sound weird, but I've been looking for a housekeeper. Do you have experience with that?"

With the number of hours Molly's mom worked after her parent's divorce? "Uh, yeah. I did most of the cleaning when I was a kid."

He gave her another fantastic smile. "Great. Uh, I don't have a ton of time. I'm supposed to be meeting a client in twenty minutes." He pulled a card out from his pocket. "Here, that's my number. If you can start tomorrow, that would be great."

She took the card and studied it. "You haven't brutally murdered anyone, have you?"

"Maybe it's just me, but I tend to follow the Judeo-Christian ethic of 'Thou shall not kill.'"

Her mouth dropped open. "No way. *So I Married an Axe Murderer?*"

His smile widened. "Really? No one has ever gotten that."

"It's one of my favorite movies."

Taking the card from her, he whipped out a pen and quickly wrote on it. "That's my address. I leave for work around eight thirty, so if you could be there a little earlier than that, that would be awesome."

"The power of that movie never ceases to amaze me," she whispered.

He laughed. "Yeah, me too." Sticking his pen back in his pocket, he checked his watch. "Oh, geez, I have to go. I'll see you tomorrow."

Molly watched as he waited for a car to pass and then jogged across the street. He was attractive, sweet, and he knew one of her favorite movies. If she wasn't already dating someone, she'd be turning down the job offer and hoping he'd ask her out. Not that an employee couldn't date their boss, but with the way things were in this day and age, you had to be careful with that.

Still, she had a new job working for a nice man. A very hot nice man. Grumbling to herself, she stuck his card in her purse and stood. She needed to get home, find some clothes that were good for cleaning, and make sure she got to his apartment on time the next morning. Tomorrow was going to be awesome.

CHAPTER 1

Six months later...

CLOSING HIS EYES, Josiah rolled his shoulders, trying to ease the tension that had built over the course of the day. Bringing work home over the weekend had been a chore, but it was necessary if he planned to go home for the holidays in three weeks.

Instead of spending his Saturday doing something fun, he was scouring available commercial properties. His newest client was a prominent figure in the Dallas community, Malakai Raven, the lead singer of Crush. Finding him the perfect place for a restaurant and making him happy could potentially boost Josiah's career. Not potentially—it would definitely get him closer to winning the Realtor of the Year award and a commercial realtor award as well.

Not that he really needed it. He and his brothers liked to play the lottery, and three years ago, they'd become billionaires overnight. Thirty years old, and if he wanted, he'd never have to work another day in his life.

That wasn't going to happen, though. His parents believed in hard work, and they'd instilled it in him and his siblings: Bear, Hunter, Wyatt, and Carrie Anne. His own desire to show that he could be successful pushed him too. Yeah, the money was great, but it did nothing to show that Josiah was accomplished. And that was something he wanted more than anything—his parents' respect.

"Long day?" asked his housekeeper, Molly Hines. With her head tilted, her short dark hair just barely touched her shoulders.

Man, she was beautiful, but he'd thought that since the moment he saw her. Six months ago, on a whim, he'd hired her after witnessing her manager firing her in front of an entire coffee shop. To Josiah, that was a horrible way to treat someone, and when he'd found her crying, he'd offered her a job cleaning his apartment.

At first, he'd thought about asking her out, but he'd learned shortly after she started working for him that she had a boyfriend. All notions of dating were gone at that point. He wasn't the kind of guy to steal a girl.

He'd thought about asking if she was still seeing the guy, but he'd chicken out every time. What if she got offended? He didn't want her to quit because he was too nosey.

Josiah stood, yawned loudly, and stretched. "Oh, I'm sorry. I think I lost track of time."

Her eyebrows knitted together. "You work too hard, Mr. West."

No matter how hard he tried to get her to call him Josiah, she wouldn't, and she was only a year younger than him. Mr. West it was, and every time she called him that, it made him want to look for his dad, King. "Maybe, but I want to go home for the holidays with a clear calendar."

He followed her into the living room and watched as she slipped on her coat she'd draped over the couch. She held up a finger. "Oh, before I forget. I've been meaning to ask about your holiday plans."

"Yeah, I guess I need to let you know about that. I'll be leaving Dallas the day before Thanksgiving and most likely won't be back until the first of the year.

Knowing my mom, I won't be given a choice." He chuckled.

Molly's lips turned down ever so slightly. "Oh, okay. I don't think you'll need me if you're not here."

"Uh." He scratched the back of his neck. He'd not thought that through, and he hated seeing the little frown. If she wasn't working, she wouldn't get paid. Maybe he could give her a bonus closer to Thanksgiving. "Well…"

She waved him off as she walked to the front door. "It's okay, Mr. West. I'm fine."

That was her typical response. In the last few weeks, he'd noticed not only was she saying it a lot more, but something was different about her too, like the dark circles around her eyes. He'd wanted to ask about it, but he'd felt awkward inquiring about her home life.

He walked her to the door. "Molly, I hope you know that if you need anything, you can just ask. I mean, I don't want to pry, but..."

Her posture softened. "You really are wonderful to me already, and I couldn't ask for a better boss. I'm fine, really, but I appreciate your kindness."

"All right. I guess I'll see you next time?"

"Bright and early Tuesday." She beamed and waved bye.

He closed the door and leaned his back against it. With a heavy sigh, he pushed off and went to his small kitchen. Again, it was dinner for one.

It was times like these when he felt the loneliness the most. No family. No girlfriend. He had friends, but Luke Barker was usually on call at the firehouse, and Case Palmer was a lawyer and even more of a workaholic than Josiah.

After a look through the barren fridge, he rifled through one of the cabinet drawers and pulled out a stack of brochures for delivery places. Pizza. Thai. Asian Fusion. Irish-Italian. He needed to get a dartboard, pin the menus, and pick one that way. At least it would be more fun.

He closed his eyes and blindly lifted one up. A quick peek with one eye, and he shook his head. "Meh. Not that one." A few more blind picks, and he was ordering tacos with some chips and queso. Hopefully, the cheese wouldn't be a solid brick by the time it arrived...like last time.

Just as he flopped down on the couch, his phone rang. "Really?" He wasn't sure what frustrated him more. The fact that he'd forgotten his phone in the kitchen, or that he'd just sat down and had to get up again. He stood and jogged to the kitchen, answering the call on the last ring. "Hello?"

"Hey, bud." His dad's deep voice filtered out.

Josiah put the phone on speaker and walked back to the couch. "Hey, Dad. What's up?" The last part of the sentence came out in a rush as he flopped down.

His dad chuckled. "Oh, you know your mom. She's dividing and conquering the holidays. I'm making sure you've made plans to be here."

"Yeah, I'll be there."

"She made me promise to ask if you're bringing anyone."

Rolling his eyes, Josiah's shoulders sagged. "If I lie, will she kill me?"

His dad snorted and coughed. "She'd kill us both. You for lying and me for knowing it."

Josiah laughed. "No, I'm not bringing anyone. It'll just be me."

"I told your mom she needed to be happy with the three that are already married off. You and Bear will find your other half when it's time."

"At least I'm not actively trying to avoid it like Bear."

Another deep chuckle rumbled from his dad. "Well, to be fair to your brother, his last girlfriend would have put me on the no-date list too. Then Carrie Anne conspiring with Bandit to put him on a dating website…if I was Bear, I'd be finding a cave to hide in at this point."

His dad had a point. Poor Bear. When he found out their sister had roped Bandit into putting his profile on Mr. Matchmaker, Bear had wanted to strangle both her and Bandit.

Carrie Anne had struck a bargain with Bear to at least try one date. He'd relented, and the date had been a disaster. The way Bear told it, swimming with hungry sharks would have been more fun.

"I don't have time to date right now, Dad." After setting his phone on his chest, Josiah stuffed his hands behind his head as he stretched out. Plus, the women he knew were into art galleries and lobster dinners. He wanted a girl who loved pizza, popcorn with milk duds in it, and movie nights.

"Sure you do. You just chose not to," his dad replied.

"I guess." His whole family knew about his last relationship. They'd been on friendly terms, and he'd seen it going somewhere. Until he figured out she knew about his lottery winnings.

It was easy to forget what was in his bank account. His apartment was the same as before he won, his lifestyle was the same, and everything else for that matter.

He was still the same guy driving the pre-owned blue F-150. Granted, he'd had it painted, but it wasn't new.

"Look, bud, I know the last one wasn't so great, but there are a lot of good women out there. Dip your toe in. It might not be as bad as you think."

Josiah nodded. "I know, Dad, and I will. Maybe after the holidays, I'll see how warm the water is." He chuckled.

The doorbell rang, and he looked over his shoulder. "Oh, hey, Dad, that's delivery. I need to get that. Tell Mom, yes, I'll be there, and I'm staying until the new year."

"Okay, bud, see you in a few weeks."

Josiah ended the call and rushed to the door. As he signed for the food, he thought over his conversation with his dad. Maybe he was right. This whole meal-for-one business was getting old. He'd go home for the holidays, get some rest, and return to the city refreshed and ready to give dating another go.

Maybe.

He shut the door and dug into the bag, pulling out a taco. Yep, women were smart enough not to order tacos from the same place that sold sushi. Better, they were bright enough not to keep the menu and then blindly pick it.

At this rate, he'd need a woman just to keep from giving himself food poisoning. A second-long debate had him dumping the bag in the trash and grabbing his keys. This time next year, maybe life would be different.

CHAPTER 2

With a toss, Molly's keys clinked as they hit the metal dish sitting on the kitchen counter, and she shrugged out of her coat. "I'm home."

The babysitter walked into the tiny living room, holding Ellie. "She's such a good baby."

Weren't all babies good babies? Maybe *easier* was a better word, and Molly was thankful for that. Oh, she still woke up every few hours to eat, as evidenced by the dark circles around Molly's eyes. Ellie was worth it, though. That little smile, those kissable sweet cheeks, and her tiny fingers as they wrapped around Molly's finger and her heart. This tiny bundle of joy was worth everything to Molly.

She took Ellie from Lisa and smiled down at her. "Hey, you."

Sinking onto the couch, Molly cradled Ellie and stared at her in wonder. When her brother, Derek, showed up four months ago with Brenda, his pregnant girlfriend, in tow, asking for Molly's help to put the baby up for adoption, she'd been stunned.

First, her brother had spent most of his life in and out of jail. After he stole Molly's credit card, she'd cut off all contact. She'd almost told him to go away, until his girlfriend came into the frame of Molly's doorway. At that point, it wasn't just him; it was the girl he'd knocked up. Molly just wasn't tough enough to send her away—which meant three people living in her matchbox apartment.

They'd looked at several agencies, but the more Molly helped, the more she wanted the baby. At first, her brother wasn't so sure it was a good idea to give a baby to a single woman with a housekeeping job, but Molly had made the argument that at least he'd have peace that the baby would be loved. Wasn't that what mattered?

Eventually, they'd agreed with her, and three weeks ago, Eloise Grace Hines was born. Ellie cooed and hiccupped, and Molly smiled. This wasn't how she'd planned to start her family, but sometimes plans got changed. For the better.

Molly tapped Ellie lightly on the nose and then kissed her little cheek. She was the most perfect little human being Molly had ever seen. Head of blonde hair, blue eyes, and the most adorable chubby cheeks.

Lifting her gaze to Lisa, Molly said, "Thank you for staying a little late. Mr. West is going home for the holidays, so he won't need me. I figured I'd go ahead and start putting in applications."

"If he's as nice as you say, I bet if you told him you need to work, he'd help." Lisa crossed the room and took her coat from the hook by the door. She stuffed her arms into the thick knee-length coat and picked up her purse. "It wouldn't hurt to at least ask."

Mr. West was more than nice. Josiah. Just his name was like cotton candy on her tongue. He was flat-out dreamy. Just a hair taller than her with thick dark hair, blue eyes, and a smile that could bring a woman to her knees. And that deep voice? Holy macaroni, was it ever yummy.

The bow on top of that neatly bundled present of a man was that he was as kind as he was good-looking. She knew he'd only given her the housekeeping job because he caught her crying after she was fired from the coffee shop. The first day she'd arrived, she'd been suspicious because the messes were just too…neat? She had a big brother, and she knew what a real one looked like.

As wonderful as Josiah was, now that Molly had Ellie, dating was on the back burner. It had been a sign when her boyfriend dumped her. In passing, she'd mentioned thinking about adopting her brother's baby. That was all it took. He was "too young to be a dad," and if she was going to pursue that, she'd be doing it without him.

Molly didn't want Ellie to see her go through one boyfriend after another like Molly had done as a child with her own mother. All those men, in and out of Molly's life, had been hard. Just when she would think things were settled, her mom's relationship would end. From the time she was five until about nine, her world was rocked more times than she could count. Then her mom met her stepdad, and Molly loved him. After he married her mom, he'd adopted her and her brother. Even so, it didn't change all the heartache she'd endured, and Molly didn't want that for Ellie.

"I really can't ask him for more work," Molly said.

Lisa opened the door and paused. "I really think you should tell him. It would make life a little easier." With that, she shut the door, leaving Molly alone with Ellie.

Easier, but she'd feel rotten telling him, especially when she knew he didn't really need her cleaning his apartment. She made a decent wage. Enough to pay her rent, food, and take care of Ellie. That's all she really needed anyway.

Now she just needed another job while Mr. West went home for the holidays.

CHAPTER 3

Three weeks later, Wednesday of Thanksgiving week, Josiah stood in his office holding an envelope in one hand and several hundred-dollar bills in the other, trying to decide how much money Molly would take without a fight. He knew she wouldn't take pay without having earned it, but Christmas bonuses didn't count, right?

He jerked his head up as he heard the door open. "Oh, man." It was decision time.

"Mr. West?" Her voice carried through the apartment. "I'm sorry I'm late."

"Uh, that's okay." He stuffed some bills in the envelope and put the leftover in his slacks' pocket. "I'm still packing."

As he reached the doorway, he nearly ran into her.

"Oh, I'm so sorry." Her eyes went wide, and she stumbled. "I should have looked first."

He steadied her and smiled. "It's okay. I think this one's on me."

Stepping back, she tucked a silky lock of hair behind her ear. "I'll get out of your way so you can pack." She looked around his apartment. "Mr. West, nothing's dirty. I'm not really sure you need me today."

Geez, he'd been so wrapped up in figuring out her Christmas bonus, he'd forgotten to mess the place up. "That's all right. It's good you're here." He handed her the envelope filled with cash. "I won't be here for Christmas, and I wanted to make sure you got your bonus."

Her fingers brushed his as she took it, and his heart skipped a beat as a zing of energy lit up his arm. An electrical fence wouldn't have shocked him as much. Whew, he definitely needed to date a little more when he returned to Dallas next year. Or maybe by the next year, he'd have the guts to ask Molly about her relationship status.

Molly opened the envelope and gasped. "Mr. West, this is entirely too much money."

He shook his head. "No, it's not. It's a Christmas bonus. Those don't count."

A single eyebrow went up, and she leaned back. "You already pay me really well. I can't accept this."

"Yes, you can. I just gave it to you. That's how this works." He gave her a cheesy grin.

Her lips rolled in, and her cheeks lifted as she tried to hide her smile. "What am I going to do with you?"

"Uh…" Kiss him?

He nearly choked on the thought. He'd never been happier to have a filter in his life. If that had actually tumbled from his lips, he would've been looking for a hole to hide in and possibly a new housekeeper.

Taking a deep breath, she shook her head. "You're a very sweet man. It makes no sense to me why you're still single." She quickly put her fingers to her mouth. "I meant…" She sagged a little. "I'm so sorry. That was a weird thing to say. I just meant you're too nice to be alone."

Josiah slipped his hands into his pants pockets, hanging his head so she didn't catch him blushing. "I appreciate the compliment." He turned and stopped on his way out of the room. "I guess I'll go finish packing."

"Is there something you need me to do?"

"I have some laundry that needs folded, but other than that, I need you to have a great holiday. Take some of that and pamper yourself. Okay?" He glanced at her and smiled. "Merry Christmas, Molly."

"You too, Mr. West..." She mumbled something under her breath, but he couldn't quite make it out.

He walked into his bedroom and grabbed a few more of his toiletries he'd used earlier that morning. With those packed, he zipped his suitcase and stood there a second, trying to think of anything he might have forgotten.

The doorbell rang, startling him. Why would anyone be coming by to see him when they knew he was leaving town? He walked to the living room, pulling his luggage behind him, just as Molly walked in from the laundry room.

"I have no idea who that could be," Josiah said as he crossed the room and opened the door.

A distraught woman holding a car seat with a crying baby covered in a pink blanket stood in front of him. "Uh..."

"Is Molly here?" The question came out in a rush. "I..."

He turned and nearly ran into Molly for the second time that day. "There's a lady looking for you."

"Molly, I'm so sorry, but I have to leave early today. My mom fell down the stairs. I just got a call from the service, and they're rushing her to the hospital." She quickly stepped forward, handed the baby to Molly, and waved as she rushed away. "I'm so sorry. I'll call you."

Josiah's eyebrows shot up. "I feel I may not have been as observant as I should have. You have a baby?"

Molly took the wailing infant out of the car seat and cradled her in an effort to soothe her. "I'm so sorry."

He held out his hands. "Let me try."

She hesitated a moment before giving him the baby.

He gently rocked her back and forth and smiled. "Hey, what's all this ruckus?" he asked softly. "You're too pretty to cry." The longer he talked to her, the less she cried, until she settled down.

"Wow, you're really good," Molly said.

He glanced up at her as the baby wrapped her tiny hand around his index finger. "Yeah, my mom tells me I'm wasting my power by not being a politician."

Molly laughed. "I'm really sorry for all this. I promise it won't happen again."

"It's okay." Josiah continued to rock the little one. "What's her name?"

"Eloise Grace. I call her Ellie for short." With her soft blonde hair and blue eyes, her name most definitely fit her. This little person in his arms was the most perfect little person on the planet. Well, next to his nephew Travis.

With another quick glance up, he said, "I like that name. It fits her. How old is she?"

Molly blinked a few times. "Six weeks tomorrow."

Josiah didn't think she could be much older than that. "She's precious."

"Okay, why are you not married? Do you have some growth I'm unaware of, or…what? Because I can't figure you out."

With a snort, Josiah shook his head. "I'm told I haven't found the right woman yet." He stroked Ellie's cheek with his finger. "I've just been busy, and…" What could he say? That he was too chicken to date after being used the last time? Or did he tell her he was desperate to make his family proud of him and he was too busy to date? "I've really got no better answer than that."

Ellie gurgled and little bubbles formed on her lips. It wouldn't take him but a second to fall head over heels for this little girl. Who wouldn't? "Man, she's just amazing. I didn't know you were even pregnant."

She hesitated a second. "I wasn't."

He looked at her and blinked. "Huh?" That was the best he could come up with? Huh?

She softened and took a deep breath. "My brother

got his girlfriend pregnant, and they were going to put her up for adoption. I couldn't let them do it. I mean, I know I'm not perfect, but I knew I'd take care of her and love her, so I adopted her."

A newfound respect for Molly filled his heart. "That's a pretty big sacrifice." He looked back down at Ellie, her little smile and big eyes turning him to mush.

"But so worth it."

"I can't disagree." He looked up at Molly and smiled. "A beautiful single woman with an equally adorable baby. And you're asking me how I'm still single?"

"Most men don't think like you." She reached her arms out to take the baby, and he reluctantly handed Ellie back to Molly. "Besides, I don't really want to date. I need to focus on her, and a relationship right now just isn't a great idea. Maybe when she's older."

Oddly enough, that hit Josiah hard. He'd thought of asking her out a few times, but he just couldn't. Aside from the fact that he thought she was dating someone this whole time, he was her employer. A boss asking the housekeeper for a date made him feel uncomfortable. What if she took it wrong? "I can see your point." Now he was glad he didn't ask. If she'd said no, who knew how long it would've taken to muster up the courage to ask someone else.

With a heavy sigh, she moved toward the couch. "Let me get my coat on, and I'll let you go so you can head home."

"Are you going to be spending the holidays with your parents? I'd guess they'd be thrilled to see her."

Molly shook her head. "You'd guess wrong. I don't have a bad relationship with my parents, but we're not the Brady Bunch. Most likely, they won't even be in town."

His mouth fell open. "But you do have family to spend the holidays with, right?"

"No," she said just above a whisper.

That wasn't going to work for Josiah. "Come spend them with my family."

She vehemently shook her head. "Oh, no. I couldn't. You've been wonderful, and I can't do that."

How could he get her to accept the invitation? "It's not about you. It's about Ellie. Shouldn't her first Christmas be spent with a houseful of people?"

Her lips pinched together, and she glared at him. "I'm more than enough for Ellie."

Whoops. That had not gone as planned. "No, I mean, you're more than enough. That's not what I'm saying."

"Then what *are* you saying?" she asked, her eyes narrowing a little further.

"That if you come home with me, maybe my mom will be too focused on Ellie to ask me about my dating life." Dude. He'd pulled that out of nowhere, but, man, that was a slam dunk of an excuse worthy of a high-five. With the recent birth of Gabby's baby boy, it would be one baby for each grandparent. It would be perfect.

Molly chuckled and shook her head. "Just how much real estate do you sell? With that kind of charm, I'm thinking it's a lot."

"I do okay, but," he held up a finger, "I wasn't kidding about my mom. My sister is married, and both my brothers Wyatt and Hunter are married. That leaves me and Bear."

She held his gaze a moment. "So you're asking me because you want to use Ellie to keep your mom from bugging you about dating?"

"When you put it like that, it sounds bad, but yes." That wasn't totally true. Yes, his mom would go wild over Ellie, but he liked Molly. Having her around for the holidays would be a plus in his book. "So, willing to bail me out?"

Molly lowered her gaze to Ellie and inhaled deeply. "It *would* be nice for her to have her first Christmas surrounded by people. Way better than my little one-bedroom apartment." She lifted her head. "I don't know, Mr. West. I feel like I'm taking advantage of you. I don't feel right about it."

Josiah wanted to knock himself over the head with a frying pan. Women! Arguing with one was akin to telling a river to stop running. Neither listened. "You aren't, but…if it will help, you can clean the house while you're there." Not that any of his family would let her lift a finger, but what she didn't know wouldn't hurt him…yet.

When she didn't answer, he pulled from the Flynn Rider school of thought and hit her with a smolder. "Please?"

With a gasp, her mouth dropped open. "You just Flynn-Ryder smoldered me. That is *not* okay."

For a second, he froze. He'd never been called on it before, and in a way, he was kinda impressed that she did. "In my defense, you did leave me no choice. A man has to do what a man has to do."

Molly giggled, and Ellie cooed. "You're not going to take no for an answer, are you?"

Josiah shook his head. "Once you meet my mom, you'll understand just how dire my circumstances are." He slipped his finger into one of Ellie's hands. "Besides, Ellie likes me. I can read babies, and she's totally telling you to save me."

"Your mom's right. You're wasting your powers.

I'm just not sure if they're good or evil." She grinned and sighed. "All right. I think it would be good for Ellie to have a nice Christmas. But," she said, pointing her finger at him, "I'm cleaning house while I'm there. You got it?"

Oh, he got it, and he'd get it even worse when they got to Caprock Canyon and there was no housework to do, but it was worth it. His mom would be so starry-eyed for Ellie and Travis that Josiah and Bear wouldn't even be on the radar. Shoot, Bear would probably give him half the ranch for that.

The holidays had just gone from miserable to awesome.

CHAPTER 4

Molly stopped at her apartment door and stuck her key in the lock. She turned to Josiah. It felt so odd to call him that, but he'd made a good point that they couldn't go through the holidays with her calling him Mr. West. Every male on the West side of the family would be responding.

"Is something wrong?" he asked and looked down at the car seat he was holding. "She's still sleeping soundly." He glanced back up innocently as if to say he was capable of handling her.

At least he hadn't used the smolder against her again. He'd seemed amazed she'd known what he was doing. As gorgeous as he was, using that against a defenseless woman just wasn't right. How was she supposed to keep things professional? Especially since now she was mixing even more pleasure with business by going to his hometown with him.

"No, nothing's wrong. I just..." Why had she said he could come with her while she packed? He'd see where she lived, and while it wasn't rat-infested, it wasn't a nice apartment like his. Not until they reached the front door did she suddenly become conscious of it.

"Just what?"

Aside from the fact that he'd already spent money on her and Ellie, she was worried about going home with him. What if his family didn't like her? Just because he was nice didn't mean his whole family was, despite his reassurance to the contrary.

"Molly?"

She chewed on her lip. "I'm..."

He held her gaze, his blue eyes seeming to bore straight through her. "Your apartment doesn't define your abilities as a mother, if that's what you're worried about. At least, I don't think so."

Molly rolled her lips in and quickly turned to face the door again, blinking back tears. He'd read her mind. Not that she thought she wasn't providing for Ellie well enough; just...people could be so judgmental. She unlocked the door and stepped inside, holding it so Josiah could walk in.

"Are you sure you're okay waiting for me to pack?" Molly asked as she flipped the light on.

"I'm fine. We're in no rush." He smiled.

That smile. It had to be the most perfect smile she'd ever seen, aside from Ellie's, of course, and she was going to be spending the holidays with it. And those lips. A set of the most perfectly kissable lips ever…that belonged to her boss. Maybe on the road to Caprock Canyon, he'd do something disgusting and kill every fantasy she'd been having since she started working for him six months ago.

When she adopted Ellie, she'd made a promise to put dating on hold. Josiah was the first man to test that resolve. How he was still single was a mystery she couldn't figure out.

"What?" he asked, his head tilting.

She startled as she realized she'd been staring at him. Shaking her head to clear her thoughts, she said, "Nothing. Let me pack. I'll be quick."

"Sure," he replied, taking a seat on the couch.

Molly hurried into her bedroom and dug in her closet for a suitcase. In the very far corner, buried under comic books and well-read books, she found a soft-side suitcase that had seen better days. It would have to do.

She pulled it out and dropped it on the bed. Should

she ask him what she should bring? Or should she pack a few different things and hope for the best? Option two sounded good. With her mind made up, she darted around the room, throwing stuff in until she got to the toiletries. Half a bottle of shampoo? It would have to do. Once she had everything together, she lugged it back into the living room.

He lifted his gaze and patted Ellie's diaper bag sitting next to him. "I figured while you were packing, I'd get her stuff together."

Wow. He'd just done it. No asking at all. "Thank you. I'll need to stop on the way and pick up some more formula." She crossed the small area and unzipped the bag. "Not that I don't trust you; I just need to double-check."

"I get it. Some weird guy packing stuff. It's not like I'm Mary Poppins." He stood and rubbed the back of his neck. "You've got three diapers left."

He began to speak again, and she pointed her finger at him. "I know what you're about to say, and I can buy them. You've already gone above and beyond." She zipped the diaper bag up. "How do you know all this stuff about babies?"

"That's how I made extra money when I was a kid. It started with me watching my two younger siblings and went from there."

Well, that made sense. "I guess stock boy wasn't your thing?"

Chuckling, he shook his head. "No." He picked up the car seat. "I guess we have everything. Are you ready?"

"Are you sure this is a good idea? Maybe I should just stay home." She couldn't believe she'd agreed in the first place. That smolder must have had more power than she first thought.

His shoulders sagged, and the corners of his lips quirked down. "I really wish you would." Puppy dog eyes? That was worse than a smolder. How could a man so sweet be so diabolical?

"Don't you give me those sad eyes. That's not fair."

"What?"

She groaned and leveled her eyes at him. "Really?"

He shrugged, shooting her a half-smile. "I believe we've had this conversation already. A man has to do—"

"What a man has to do." She finished his sentence. "Your mom and I are going to have a serious talk about your powers. Wielding them on unsuspecting people is wrong."

A chuckle rumbled from his chest. "In all seriousness, my family will love you, and you won't regret coming. I promise. Don't second-guess yourself.

You're a great mom, and Ellie will be loved on to her heart's content."

Molly nodded. She did want that for Ellie. "Thank you. I guess we'll come."

His face lit up. "Sure. You ready?"

Nope. She sure wasn't, but she suspected he'd cry if she backed out. Okay, maybe not cry, but one more puppy dog look, and no court on earth would hold her responsible for kissing him. It was going to be a long, long holiday season.

∽

Two hours later, and they were just getting out of Dallas. They'd been caught in the rush hour traffic. Molly had quickly recanted her opposition to the car seat as vehicles zipped by, changing lanes like they were in a live version of *The Fast and the Furious*. She'd braced her hands on the dash several times because he'd slammed the brakes to avoid hitting someone more than once. It was harrowing, to say the least.

Now, out of the heart of the city, there was still traffic; it just wasn't as crazy. "Is it just me, or was that really bad traffic today?" Molly asked.

He grunted a laugh. "It wasn't just you."

"And the car seat…maybe you were right," she mumbled the last part of the sentence.

Cupping his ear with his hand, he said, "I'm sorry. What did you say?"

Molly lightly smacked him on the arm. "You heard me."

"Yes, but my ego needs you to speak a little louder." He chuckled and lifted his chin to look in the rearview mirror. "I'm glad we got the rear-facing mirror. I like being able to check on Ellie."

Going to the store with him was more like shopping with a five-year-old. *No* was not his favorite word at all. The man could pout like a pro. Along with formula and diapers, they got a host of things Ellie just had to have. A toy for her car seat, a couple of warm onesies, a hat—because her little ears would get cold— and the mirror. Oh, and a teddy bear. All little girls needed a teddy bear. Apparently, that was a rule Molly was unaware of.

"Thank you for the onesies and stuff. I just feel bad you keep spending money on us," Molly said.

With a shrug, he said, "This is my love language, apparently. I mean, not that I love you or that…" He groaned and scratched the back of his neck. Josiah had to be the cutest man on the earth. The way the tips of his ears turned pink when he was embarrassed was adorable.

"I know what you mean, but what made you read the love language book? Are…are you dating someone?" Did she want to know the answer to that? She steadied herself for the response in case it was something she didn't want to hear.

"Um, no. I'm not dating anyone." He paused a beat before continuing. "I read it because I wanted to understand my clients and myself better. Actually, I read a lot. I have a couple of friends, Luke and Case, but that's about it. We get together when we can, but they're both busy too. It makes for being alone a lot."

Reads a lot? He'd spoken her language. "Me too. Well, before I had Ellie."

"What do you like to read?" He shot her a crooked smile, and her brain felt liquefied. *Now* there was competition for which smile was his best.

She held in a groan and chastised herself. He was her boss. Her good-looking, adorable, likes-to-read boss. Her pep talks were about as good as her window-cleaning. Terrible.

"Uh, just about anything. I loved *The Princess Bride, The Outsiders, Lord of the Rings, Ender's Game—*"

Josiah sucked in a sharp breath. "That's my favorite book. Man, I love it. I think I've read it, oh man, I don't know how many times. I had a paperback copy that I literally wore out. To the point that it started falling apart."

Molly twisted in the seat, leaning her back against the door. "Have you read the sequels? I liked them, but there was just something about *Ender's Game* that grabbed me."

"Yeah, and I kinda felt the same way. I think that's how things are, though. Nothing is ever as good as the first."

"Except for the second *Sharknado* movie. That one rocked."

He shot her a quick glance, his entire face lit up. "What? No way! You like those movies too? I'm always ribbed because I love them. They're hysterical."

Molly was stunned. So, this hot guy with the killer smile loved to read *and* loved *Sharknado*? She secretly pinched herself because there was no way this dreamy dude could ever have that much in common with her.

Her no-dating rule stank, but she just couldn't do that to Ellie. Josiah could be awesome a year, maybe two, possibly even three, but what if things got rough? She'd thought her last relationship was solid too. He'd wanted kids, loved the same things she did, and what did he do? Ellie wasn't his, and he wasn't sticking around. She couldn't risk putting her daughter through that over and over. Not when Molly had firsthand experience of how hard it was.

She did have one question for him. "Did you hire me because you felt sorry for me that I got fired at that coffee shop?"

He inhaled and cleared his throat. "Uh…I plead the fifth."

"I knew it."

His jaw dropped open. "You did not. I completely trashed my apartment."

Molly lifted an eyebrow. "Really? I have a slob for an older brother, and his room was putrid. I'm surprised the space station wasn't using nose pins, the smell was so terrible." That was the funniest part of Josiah hiring her. She'd started that first day, and all his clothes smelled surprisingly fresh…like someone had just washed and dried them.

Josiah opened and closed his mouth a few times and then shifted in his seat a little.

"You have how many siblings?" she asked.

"Uh, four." He glanced at her. "Why?"

She laughed. "You were the weakest link when came to secrets, weren't you?" She could see him working not to smile, and she laughed harder. "Oh, yeah, I'm so right."

He huffed. "I will break out the big guns if you

don't watch it. I have all kinds of moves up my sleeve. Like, I wear extra-large shirts just to hold them all."

Molly palmed her forehead and let out an exaggerated sigh. He was cute, charming, and witty. Whatever else he had up his sleeves…well, if it worked as well as all the other stuff he'd done so far, she was going to be undone by the time the new year arrived.

CHAPTER 5

*A*fter topping off the gas tank, Josiah parked in front of the convenience store. One of the reasons he'd stopped in Wichita Falls was because he was positive there'd be a clean bathroom in case Molly needed it.

Molly unbuckled herself and turned in the seat, checking on Ellie. "She's awake and I'd bet wet." A few minutes later, Molly faced forward, cradling what had to be the most precious baby ever.

Of course, that was just Josiah's opinion, but he was confident he was right. He reached out for Ellie. "I'll stay here with her while you use the restroom. I don't think she should go in there. Not this time of year."

"You just want to hold her, don't you?" Molly asked, pressing a kiss to Ellie's forehead.

Shrugging, he smiled. "Guilty. Plus, seriously, this isn't a good time of the year for an infant to be going places. She needs a chance to build up her immunity."

Molly cocked her head. "I really...never mind."

"What?" he asked, holding out his arms for Ellie.

"You're too perfect."

He shook his head. "No, I'm not."

That was an understatement. He trusted too easily, loved too quickly, and, most of the time, was so socially awkward it was painful. Which was why he worked so much. Aside from the fact that he loved it, he was desperate to prove he could be just as successful as his siblings.

"I'm..." He wanted to give her the list, but he didn't want her feeling sorry for him. "Just trust me; I'm not."

Molly, on the other hand, was as close to perfect as any woman he'd ever met. She loved *Sharknado*, reading, and comics. He'd never really read any manga, but with the right motivation, he would. A motivation like a girl who was as smart as she was hot.

She narrowed her eyes. "My gut tells me that's not true, but the call of nature is now screaming." She handed Ellie to him. "I'll be back as quick as I can."

Josiah held Ellie in the crook of his arm, smiling as

Molly got out. He looked back down at Ellie. "You are too adorable for words."

The sentence was barely out of his mouth before a rumble came from the wrong end of the baby. Wow. "How can someone so small produce something so deadly? And my mouth was open." He laughed, and the baby grinned. "Yeah, I bet you do feel better. *What* has your momma been feeding you?"

He carefully laid her on the seat and reached into the back to grab the diaper bag. No way was he waiting for Molly to get back. That diaper had to go.

Digging through the bag, he pulled out a diaper, wipes, and some lotion. "Huh, stuff made just for your tiny butt." He looked from the tube to her and grinned. "Tiny but mighty."

After unsnapping her onesie, he peeled the tabs on the diaper off and blinked. He was pretty sure the smell could be the cause of an apocalypse. "Never ask if it can get any worse," he said as he wiped her clean. Once he had lotion on her, he fastened the diaper.

Just as he was finishing, Molly pulled the door open. "You changed her?"

He startled and jumped, hitting his head on the ceiling of the truck.

"I'm sorry!" Molly covered her mouth with both hands. "Are you okay?" The words came out muffled.

Josiah rubbed the top of his head and winced. "I'm okay, and, yes, I changed her. It was either that or drown in the bog of eternal stench."

She waved her hand in front of her face. "Oh, yeah, wow. Sorry. That was a bad one."

"Uh, yeah. I had no idea something so foul could come from a person so little." He finished snapping Ellie's onesie and picked her up.

Molly got in, and he handed her the baby before opening the door, jumping out, and tossing the evidence of something unholy. He jogged back and leaned into the cab. "I'm going to use the restroom and then grab some coffee. It'll be horrible, but I need it."

"Why would you say it's horrible?" She looked up from Ellie.

"My sister-in-law makes the best coffee ever known to man. I was addicted by the time I left Caprock Canyon last year, and I've craved it ever since." He smiled. "Do you want anything?"

She shook her head. "No, but thank you for changing her."

"It wasn't the most enjoyable experience, but I got a smile out of it." He grinned.

Molly's face fell. "You did not."

"I did. It was adorable too."

"Not fair. She hasn't smiled for me yet." Molly placed a few kisses on her face. "Little stinker."

Josiah liked this. Granted, a poopy diaper wasn't the highlight of the trip, but he liked the package. He wanted this one day. A woman who shared his interests, their baby, and trips home to see family and vacations to Disney World.

He took a deep breath and rolled his eyes. Just his luck. He'd met the one woman who made his pulse race, and she wasn't interested in dating. Maybe a little of the Christmas magic that helped his brothers would find a way to help him too. Not that he was holding his breath. He didn't want to pass out and crack his head on the ground.

∽

CUTTING the engine to the truck, Josiah was thrilled to finally be sitting still. He loved his family, but the drive he could do without. He'd tried to convince Bear to put in a landing strip, and he wouldn't go for it. It would spook the cattle.

"Hey," Josiah said, gently shaking Molly. "We're here."

She slowly lifted her head and yawned. "I fell asleep on you, didn't I?"

He smiled. "Yeah, but that's okay. It can be a boring drive."

"Wow. It's so dark out here. And quiet. It's like a vacuum almost." She stretched her arms in front of her and rolled her neck. "I like it."

"Yeah, I do too, but by the time the new year arrives, I'm ready to get back to Dallas." Twisting in his seat, he unbuckled Ellie and then gave her to Molly. "You carry her, and I'll grab the luggage."

She nodded. "Okay. Do you think your family waited up for you to get here?"

Shrugging, he said, "It's a tossup. If they weren't playing cards, probably not. If they did, most likely they're still up. We take card games very seriously."

Molly chewed her bottom lip as she looked at the house. "I hope they don't mind us coming."

He hadn't called anyone to let them know about Molly, but he also knew his family. Molly was going to fit in just fine. "You're kidding, right? One, you have a baby. Two, I'm bringing home a woman. Three, well, just double the first two, and that should take care of the rest of your worry." He smiled.

It didn't seem to ease the worry etched on her face, so he took her hand. "Molly, they're going to love you. The second you walk through that door, you'll pretty much be a member of the family for life."

"Okay. I just...I'm a little defective at times. I laugh at the wrong things, like the weirdest stuff...I don't know. There's a reason I don't have a lot of friends."

He grunted. "Wow, you're pretty much perfect, then."

In the dim dome light of the pickup cab, he could see her cheeks turn pink. Man, if he could just affect her like that all the time, it would be awesome. Even if she didn't want to date, she needed a friend. He'd been in that zone more than once. It wasn't the most desirable position to be in, but he could handle it. Ellie needed it too. Maybe he'd babysit from time to time so Molly could take a break and go out.

"Come on. Maybe Bandit's baked some cookies." Josiah shut the door, pulled the back door open, and grabbed the luggage. After slamming the door, he rounded the back of the pickup bed and stopped next to Molly.

Once they were inside the house, Josiah said, "I'll show you—"

"Hey!" Carrie Anne said softly as she walked into the living room. She must not have seen Molly and Ellie at first because her eyes widened as she stopped a few feet from them. "Mom is going to want an explanation."

Josiah set the luggage down. "This is a friend of

mine." He paused, trying to find a way to phrase Molly's family situation. "Her family couldn't make it into town, and I invited her to ours." Smiling, he turned to Molly. "Carrie Anne, this is Molly, and the baby she's holding is Ellie."

His sister narrowed her eyes ever so slightly, and inwardly, Josiah cringed. The meddler-matchmaker had just set her sights on him. He'd have to make it clear that Molly didn't want to date. They were just friends.

Carrie Anne stepped closer, taking a peek at Ellie. "Oh, she's beautiful."

Molly smiled. "Thanks. I think so too, but I'm biased."

Ellie gurgled and wiggled a little. Man, he loved that. Well, he loved her. It hadn't taken much. Not only did he want kids, but he cared about Molly, and they were a package deal.

"You might be biased, but you aren't wrong," Josiah said. He paused before asking, "I guess you guys weren't playing cards?"

Carrie Anne nodded. "We were until about an hour ago. I couldn't sleep and just came down to get something to drink really quick."

In a way, Josiah was glad everyone was in bed. Giving Molly a chance to get settled before they descended on her seemed like a good idea. Picking up the luggage, Josiah yawned. "I think sleep sounds like a great idea."

Molly nodded. "Yeah, I need to get Ellie changed and fed."

They followed Carrie Anne up the stairs. When they reached the second floor, she whispered just loud enough that they could hear, "Israel and I are here on the right. Mom and Dad are across the hall. Gabby's parents are staying with her and Wyatt at the orchard. Hunter and Reagan are in the room next to Mom and Dad. Bear built on to the house this past year, so he's downstairs."

Josiah's eyebrows lifted to his hairline. "Added on?" He'd had no idea Bear was doing that, but he could kind of see Bear wanting to. While he loved having the family over for the holidays, he also loved his solitude. Plus, he woke up pretty early to take care of the animals. "Wow."

Nodding, Carrie Anne replied, "Yeah, I was a little surprised, but not much. I kinda think he's still mad at me for putting him on that dating website."

"It's like you have ESPN or something." Josiah laughed.

Carrie Anne's expression was blank. "What?"

He sighed. "Never mind."

By the wide-eyed looked Molly was giving him, Josiah knew he'd need to tell her what happened. "I'll explain later," he said, leaning in.

"You're so weird." His sister yawned again. "Night. I'll see you guys in the morning." She slipped into her room and left Josiah and Molly in the hallway.

He knew his sister didn't mean the little remark as a real dig at him, but it was late, and he was tired after driving.

He tipped his head toward the rooms down the hall. "I say we take those at the end of the hallway. It'll keep down some of the noise."

She nodded and walked with him. "Your sister put your brother on a dating website?"

As he reached the room on the right, he said, "Yeah, and he was ticked. It was one of those things that was funny as long as it wasn't happening to you." He paused. "Left or right?"

"Uh, right is fine."

Josiah set his luggage down and took hers into the room, setting it on the chair near the window. "If you want, I'll go make Ellie a bottle while you change her. I bet she's hungry."

"Actually, that sounds like a good plan," Molly replied as she laid Ellie on the bed.

He slipped the diaper bag off his shoulder onto the

bed and handed Molly a diaper before fishing out the formula and bottle. "I'll put my stuff in my room and then be right back." He smiled.

Molly touched his arm. "I don't know if I've said this yet, but thank you." She slightly lifted on her toes and kissed his cheek. "You're a really great guy."

Really great guy. The worst three-word combination ever, aside from *let's be friends*. It wasn't like he could say anything. She'd been clear, and he wasn't about to challenge her on it. Ellie was priority, and he understood that. From Molly's perspective, dating would be challenging. It wasn't just her heart that could get broken anymore; it was Ellie's too.

"Sure." He smiled and walked out of the room.

At least now he had a picture of exactly what he wanted: a wife, some kids, and all the adventures that entailed. The only downside was that Molly pretty much fit his mold of perfect. Again, he'd just have to settle for friendship. Not great, but better than nothing.

CHAPTER 6

Resting her head against the back of the tub, Molly closed her eyes. She'd kissed Josiah on the cheek. It had happened before her brain even kicked in, but he'd deserved a kiss on the cheek. No, he'd deserved a real kiss for being…him.

He'd offered to feed Ellie and let her take a bath. As far as gifts go, this had to be her favorite. It had been forever since she'd taken a real, relaxing bath. Her babysitter was awesome, but Molly couldn't justify paying for an extra hour just to be leisurely.

How was the man still single? He was kind and caring and compassionate. He seemed to use his whole heart when it came to people. She'd seen the little downturn of his lips when his sister had called him weird. If Molly hadn't just met her or known she was family, she probably would have said something. Even if it was just being playful, it hurt him, and Molly didn't like that at all.

The world needed more weird guys like Josiah. The kind who changed a baby's toxic poopy diapers and let their moms take baths. All without complaint or begrudging the inconvenience. He just…offered. It was genuine and sweet, and her rule was being challenged every minute she spent with him.

Groaning loudly, she wiped her face with her hands. How many times had her mom cried when a relationship ended? Then she would pick up the pieces of her broken heart and start the dating process all over again. That was *not* going to be Molly's life. It was definitely not going to be Ellie's.

With the water cooling off, she decided it was time to get out. Once she was dressed, she walked across the hall and stopped in the doorway. Based on the soft snores she was hearing, he'd fallen asleep on the bed, and she guessed by the fact that he was now wearing a dark gray t-shirt and that his button-up shirt was piled on the floor next to the bed that Ellie had spit up on him.

She quietly crossed the room and peeked over his shoulder. A man had never been more attractive to her than in that moment. Josiah was curled around Ellie, and she was just as sound asleep with her hand wrapped around his finger. He'd changed her clothes, which confirmed her suspicion that Ellie spit up not only on him but herself as well.

Now she was in a quandary. Should she try to take Ellie and risk waking her or both of them up, or did she wait until Ellie woke up later, wanting to be fed? If she waited, the baby would wake up Josiah, so Molly leaned over as easily as she could and went to lift Ellie. The moment she tried, Josiah curled around her tighter.

She set her hands on her hips, chewing the inside of her cheek, trying to figure out a way to pick up Ellie without waking him up. Again, she leaned over, and Josiah stirred.

"Hey," she said. "I was going to take Ellie so you can sleep. She'll wake up in a few hours, wanting to be fed."

"Oh." He rubbed his eyes. "She's okay. Why don't you take the night and rest? I don't mind getting up with her." Like it was instinct, he looked back at Ellie and kissed her forehead.

It took work for Molly's jaw not to hit the floor. It had been more than six weeks since she'd had the luxury of a full night's sleep—encompassing the week leading up to Ellie's birth and the entire time since she came home. "Are you sure?"

Without looking up, he took Molly's hand. "You're a great mom. You deserve some rest. I've got her, and I promise I won't let anything happen to her."

Tears pooled in her eyes, and she paused before answering, "Okay. Thank you." She turned, walked to the door, and took a quick look back before walking across the hall.

If she didn't watch it, before this trip was over, she'd fall for him. She'd known he was kind and generous, and now he was adding to her growing list of things she liked about him.

Charming, funny, sweet, and loving. Unfortunately, many of the guys her mom had dated fell into that category too. Molly would get attached and then be crushed when they left, never to be seen again. Oh, they always promised to keep in touch, but none of them had. That's not the life she wanted for her daughter. Molly didn't want Ellie to ever question the adults in her life and their love for her. Having to question that had made Molly grow up too quickly. Her plan for Ellie's future was for her to be a kid for as long as possible.

Molly liked Josiah, but she loved Ellie. Making the

choice to adopt her meant putting her first, and that was exactly what Molly was going to do too.

~

Sunlight hit Molly's face as she turned over, facing the window. It was enough of a shock that she bolted upright. How long had it been since she'd seen the sun when she woke up? The better question was, what time was it? She quickly grabbed her phone, and her eyes widened.

Noon.

Noon? It was a good thing Josiah's family ate Thanksgiving Dinner later in the day, or she'd have missed it. She dropped her phone and scrambled out of bed, rushing out of the room and into Josiah's… empty room. Where was he? Where was Ellie? She raked her hand through her hair, and just as she started to race out of his room, she paused. Josiah had Ellie. If there was one thing Molly was confident about, it was that Josiah would keep her safe.

Closing her eyes, she sucked in a lungful of air and let it out slowly. It was so strange to have someone helping her that it took her brain a second to catch up. Sheesh, not only did she need to keep her wits when it came to Josiah, but she needed to remember that all this help wasn't going to last. The start to the new year was going to be hard on her.

"Hey, Happy Thanksgiving!" Josiah said as he strolled into his room with Ellie. "Did you sleep well?" His eyebrows knitted together, and he tilted his head. "Are you okay?"

She nodded and cast her gaze to the floor. "Yeah, it took me a second to realize Ellie was with you. I haven't had her long, but I guess I'm used to taking care of her alone."

He stepped closer and held Ellie out to her. "I'm sorry. I didn't think about that."

Molly took her and smiled down at her. "Hi." She nuzzled Ellie with her nose and kissed her. When she looked up, Josiah's shoulders were sagging.

"I should have…left you a note or something. I'm really sorry."

Unlike her last boyfriend, Josiah meant it when he said he was sorry. It was completely endearing. "It's okay. Really. Thank you for letting me sleep in. How was she last night?"

"She was awesome." A smile lit up his face. Not only was he bad at keeping secrets, but she'd wipe the floor with him if they ever played poker. He was just so cute. It must have been a long night. "Don't take this the wrong way, but I've noticed you looking a little tired for a while. I thought you could use the rest."

Molly grinned. "I did, and it was amazing. The bed is out-of-this-world comfortable. I don't even remember my head hitting the pillow." She handed Ellie back to him. "I think I should grab a shower, and then maybe you can introduce me to some of your family." She was eager to meet the people responsible for the incredible guy who made her knees weak.

His eyes sparkled as he took Ellie from her. "Sure. Mom has an extra stroller, so if you want, we can go for a walk. Or we can just hang out inside. I'm open for whatever."

"Okay." She raked her hand through her hair. "Maybe I can do a little cleaning or help with the food before eating."

"Uh." He winced.

She narrowed her eyes. "You had no intention of letting me work, did you?"

Josiah smiled sheepishly and shrugged. "No."

Groaning, Molly took a deep breath and palmed her cheek. "Josiah. You are…sweet. Thank you for inviting me."

"You're welcome," he replied. "I was going to change Ellie and go back downstairs, but I can wait for you."

Shaking her head, she said, "That's okay. You're home to visit with your family. I think I'll be able to find you."

He caught her gaze and held it. "I want you to know that I respect you as her mom, so if I'm doing something you don't like, just tell me."

Every time she thought Josiah couldn't get any better, he did something else that just blew her away. She stepped closer to him, placing her hand on his forearm. "I know you do. Except when it comes to car seats." She chuckled.

"I was right about that, though." He gave her a cheesy grin.

"You think you're so funny."

Their laughter tapered down, and suddenly it was hard to breathe. This adorable guy holding her little girl was the hottest thing since grilled cheese, and he was looking at her like the world had disappeared. "Molly…I…" He stepped back. "I should let you get ready. No rush, okay?"

Just as quickly as the moment started, it was over. If Molly was a betting woman, she'd have bet the farm he was about to kiss her. And if she was sincere, she'd have let him. Which meant it was a good thing he didn't.

"Thank you for helping with her." Molly curled her

fingers around his hand and squeezed. "I can't tell you how much it's meant to me to have a little break." She hung her head. "That makes me sound horrible."

He tipped her chin up with one finger, and the normally funny, goofy guy was looking at her with such intensity she nearly gulped. "No, it doesn't. You're a great mother, and she is blessed to have you. You didn't have to step up and adopt her, but you did. I think you deserve a Mom of the Year award."

Tears pooled in Molly's eyes, and Josiah gave her a one-armed hug. "I like helping, okay? If I didn't, I wouldn't have invited you. I wouldn't have offered to watch her. You're awesome…and I thought that before I knew you had Ellie. Now you're awesome with a cape." He smiled.

"'No capes!'" She laughed.

His shoulders bounced as he laughed and took his finger from her chin. "I should have known you'd come back with that."

"I think I could hold an entire conversation using movie quotes." She grinned. "Thank you." She looked down. "That barely scratches the surface of how grateful I am."

"My surface feels very scratched."

She jerked her attention up and snickered as his entire head turned beat red.

"I'm going to go now before I choke on my own foot." He walked to the door, and she followed him.

"Josiah?"

He turned, and his gaze didn't quite meet hers. "Yeah?"

"I'll see you downstairs in a few."

"Okay."

She walked into her room, shut the door, and groaned. That man. He crossed her t's, dotted her i's, and made her winded. She'd been in trouble before they got to Caprock Canyon. Now she was white-knuckling the side of a cliff, tempted to just let go.

Her head and her heart were in a mud-wrestling contest, and neither knew which end was up.

No dating. No dating. No dating. Maybe if she repeated it enough times, she wouldn't forget it.

CHAPTER 7

She'd *scratched* *his* *surface?* Inwardly, Josiah groaned. He was an idiot. Who said stuff like that to a woman? Apparently, he did because he liked the taste of leather. Or, well, whatever his house shoes were made of. Maybe terry? He looked down and then wanted to smack himself. It didn't matter how the shoe tasted, just the fact that he'd stuffed it in his mouth.

Add to it the near-kiss. If he hadn't stepped back when he did, he would've kissed her. Talk about blowing it. They still had weeks left of the holiday, and the last thing he wanted was her upset with him.

Ellie gurgled in his arms as he sat in the recliner in the living room. He smiled down at her. Every minute he spent with her, he only wanted more.

"I see you're using your baby powers," Carrie Anne said as she took a seat on the couch adjacent to him. "She's beautiful."

"Yeah, she is." He smiled.

"And you like her mom too." Carrie Anne wagged a finger at him. "A lot."

He couldn't deny that. "I do, but as a friend. Molly doesn't want to date, and I need to respect that."

Besides, he didn't want to start a relationship with Molly—*if* he could start one—unless he told her about the money. No, it didn't change him as a person, but what if it changed her?

Plus, his real estate career was his first priority. He'd helped his latest commercial client narrow down the properties that would work. When he got back to Dallas, he'd be focusing on that for a while. Not that he didn't want to help Molly—he would do that—but full-time care was something he couldn't do at the moment.

His sister lifted an eyebrow. "Doesn't want to date? Why?"

Josiah shifted Ellie to his shoulder and patted her bottom. "On the way here, she told me about growing up. Her mom divorced her dad when she was young. With all the dating, men would come in and out of her life. She doesn't want that for Ellie. I respect that. I respect her, so I'm good with friends." It was a total lie, but he figured he needed to get used to it.

"You are as terrible a liar as you are a secret keeper." Carrie Anne chuckled. "It's okay to want to date her. Show her you're not like those guys."

He shook his head. "No, I don't want to put that kind of pressure on her. She's a new mom, and that's enough to deal with as it is. As great as Ellie is, I'm not ready to be a full-time dad."

Shaking her head, his sister rolled her eyes. "You just don't want to take a risk. You've never liked taking risks."

Yeah, because any time he did, they backfired. His last relationship was a testament to that. He'd not meant to mention his lottery winnings, but he had. Instead of backing away slowly at the sign of red flags, he'd excused some of the things she said under the guise of taking a risk. "They don't work for me."

"You back down too quickly. Stand up for yourself. You have a lot to offer a woman. Just stop being so…"

"Me? The guy who just takes the lumps and doesn't say anything?" That's exactly what he was. The nice guy. The good friend. The sweet man. All great things that lead to friendships with women that went nowhere.

His sister's posture softened. "I didn't mean it like that."

Shrugging, he said, "Yeah, I know." Except she did mean it. It was always him backing down or taking the blame for things. He was stuck in the middle. All he needed was jokers to the right and clowns to the left.

Just as he was feeling sorry for himself, Josiah glanced at Ellie on his shoulder to find her sleeping peacefully. She wasn't his, but, man, how could he feel sorry for himself when such a small human being needed him. Granted, it was temporary, but he was glad to give Molly a decent break before they returned to Dallas.

He brushed his fingers down her little head and touched her cheek. How could Molly's brother not want her? Of course, that would mean that Molly wouldn't have her, but Josiah struggled to understand how any man wouldn't want this sweet baby.

Carrie Anne moved the edge of the sofa. "I'm going to get something to drink. Can I get you something?"

He shook his head. "I'm fine."

His sister hesitated and touched his knee. "You are a great guy. I…I just want to see you happy."

"I know, and I am. Molly needs a friend, and I'm okay with that." But he was less okay the more he was around her. She used movie quotes, loved animated shows and things he liked.

He'd never met a woman like that before, but he also knew she wanted someone focused on her and Ellie. Until the year was over, his goal was winning Realtor of the Year and Commercial Transaction of the Year. Once he had those, he'd be free to have a relationship.

~

Later that afternoon, Josiah pushed his plate away. "No more. I'll explode."

Just an hour ago, all the Thanksgiving dishes were piping hot and plates were piled high. Josiah and Molly were seated next to each other, and Ellie was in the living room, snoozing in a bassinette Gabby let them borrow.

Molly finished the last bite of green bean casserole on her plate and wiped her mouth. "Bandit, you make a mean green casserole."

"Th-th-thank you, but R-R-Reagan gave me some tips," Bandit replied.

Reagan shook her head. "It was delicious even before the tips."

Josiah's dad, King, sat back, rubbing his stomach.

"Bud, you seem to outdo yourself every time you cook."

"He needs to open the restaurant again. Two more families moved to Caprock Canyon just last week," Bear said. "You just need to do it."

Bandit shook his head. "N-n-no."

"Stubborn. Most stubborn man I've ever met," Bear grumbled.

With a snort, Josiah said, "Yeah, have you looked in the mirror?"

The whole family chuckled as Bear gave Josiah a dirty look.

"Shut it," Bear growled.

Molly leaned in. "This is the best Thanksgiving I've ever had."

"So, you're admitting my use of the Flynn-Ryder smolder was a good move?" Josiah chuckled.

She grinned. "No, that was still wrong, but I *am* glad you talked me into coming."

Josiah put his arm around her and hugged her to him. "I'm glad too. Just wait 'til Christmas. Bandit makes cinnamon rolls that will make you believe in angels."

More than anything, he was glad the dark circles under her eyes were lighter than they were before. Her entire countenance seemed refreshed. It made him feel good that he'd been able to help.

She hugged him around the chest. "The food is great, but mostly, I've loved how big your family is. Everyone talking and laughing and getting along." She straightened and tucked a lock of hair behind her ear. "I guess that sounds odd, huh?"

"No, it sounds like someone who likes a big family."

"Molly," Josiah's mom, Caroline, said, "our typical tradition is to go Black Friday shopping in Amarillo. Would you want to go with us? It's just us girls. We grab breakfast and then hit the stores for deals. We'd love to have you."

Pauline leaned forward where she sat at the end of the table, holding her grandson, a babbling Travis, as he played with a plastic keyring. "Yes, Molly, we'd love it."

Josiah had explained earlier when Pauline and Amos Fredricks first arrived who they were and their relationship with his family, basically part of the family. That Gabby and Stephanie were their two girls and now Gabby was married to his younger brother, Wyatt, and that Travis was their little boy.

Carrie Anne, Gabby, and Stephanie echoed their moms. "Absolutely."

Reagan, who sat across from them, nodded. "Yes, it'll be awesome."

"Uh, well…I have Ellie…"

His mom flicked her gaze from Molly to Josiah. "Why don't you and Josiah discuss it. No pressure at all. We just want you to know you're welcome." She smiled.

"Okay. Thank you. I'll think about it."

"Last year was so much fun," his mom said with a chuckle.

Reagan rolled her eyes and leveled her gaze at Molly. "They're laughing because last year at this time, I was pretending to be Hunter's fiancée."

Hunter's entire face lit up neon red. "And all of you are grateful because her coffee is the best."

Everyone at the table laughed and murmured agreements.

Hunter put his arm around Reagan. "She's the best at a lot of things."

Reagan's cheeks turned deep red, and she ducked her head, smiling. "You're married to me. You have to say that."

"No, I don't. It's the truth."

A second later, plastic keys flew across the table, and Travis giggled. Gabby waggled her finger at him. "No throwing, mister!"

He stuck his fingers in his mouth and bounced on Pauline's lap.

Little cries began to carry into the dining room, and as Josiah started to get up, Molly stopped him. "It's my turn." She smiled.

"Okay."

He watched as Molly walked out of the dining room and settled his gaze on the table. So far, this had been his best Thanksgiving ever. Maybe he could figure out a way to convince Molly she could date him or at least let him be a part of her and Ellie's life. If he could find a way to prove he wouldn't leave if things got hard, she'd be open to the idea.

His heart dipped low into his stomach. No. He'd seen her face when his mom put her on the spot. That's not what he wanted, and he didn't want her to pull away. How could he help her if she did that? It wasn't worth losing her or Ellie just because he wanted something more. He needed to settle…like he always did.

It was best for both of them if he did that. If he somehow didn't win Realtor of the Year, he'd be working for it the next year. Molly and Ellie needed someone who put them first, and until his goal was reached, he couldn't do that.

Convincing Molly to date him and then not giving

her the attention she deserved would be wrong. He didn't want to do that to her. Not when she'd seemed so sad while talking about her childhood. The right thing to do was to keep things as they were. He'd help when he could, and maybe in a year or two, they could date.

If she was still available.

He rubbed the spot over his heart. It hurt to think that, but he wasn't going to be selfish. After all, if he cared about her and Ellie, he'd want what was best for her, even if that wasn't him.

CHAPTER 8

For the first time in her life, Molly loved Thanksgiving. The food was delicious, Josiah's family was awesome, and she felt…wanted. Although, as she thought about it, wanted didn't seem to be the right word.

Her mom never made her feel unwanted, but maybe the right word was inconvenient. Molly felt loved, but at the same time, she also felt in the way of what her mom wanted. After marrying young, her mom had Derek and then her. Not long after Molly was born, her parents' marriage had started to have trouble.

More than once, Molly suspected that her mom regretted getting married and having children. She'd been kept from the dreams she'd had for herself, and her kids were constant reminders of that.

In contrast, Josiah's parents acted like having a family was the best thing to ever happen to them. They were only a couple of years older than Molly's mom, and when they looked at each other or their children, they seemed to see their lives as full and happy. Molly wasn't jealous of Josiah, but it did make her wonder what life would have been like if she'd had a similar experience.

"What's got you so deep in thought?" Carrie Anne asked.

The sound of her voice brought Molly out of her thoughts, and she smiled. "Just the holidays when I was young. They weren't like this."

Somehow, Molly had found herself talked into going Black Friday shopping while Josiah watched Ellie. They'd left while it was still dark, and now they were having lunch. From what Molly understood, this was fuel for the second round of shopping. She'd never shopped like this. When it came to Black Friday, her opinion was that it was to be avoided at all costs.

Josiah had made the argument that Ellie needed a baby monitor and a crib. That way she could safely sleep upstairs. It wasn't until Molly pulled the envelope out that she realized he'd stuffed it with way more money than the two items required. She'd texted him, and they were going to have a long talk when she got back to the ranch. His reply was sending her a text with him giving her a goofy grin. Over the last few days, as fantastic as his other smiles were, the goofy one was her favorite.

"What were they like?" asked Pauline.

All the women had gone out of their way to make Molly feel welcome and included. Talking to them felt like talking to people she'd known forever. They'd all just clicked, and Molly had no explanation.

"Well, my dad divorced my mom when I was young. I barely remember my dad. We kept in touch a while, but then he got remarried, and communication dwindled from there." She picked a little cheese from the wrapper and nibbled it. "My mom was kind of a serial dater. Not that she was trying to date a lot. It just happened. Sometimes, her boyfriends would invite us to family things, but it was always weird and awkward."

Caroline shook her head. "That's tough."

Shrugging, Molly said, "It's okay. I love my mom, and I know she worked hard to give us a good life."

"I don't doubt that at all," Josiah's mom replied with a smile.

Reagan tilted her head. "How did you meet Josiah?"

Molly chuckled and told them the whole story, including how his messes were staged. "He's a sweet guy." And one of the reasons she'd felt she could take care of Ellie, because he paid her well. Not six-bedroom-mansion well, but comfortable, especially given the fact that she hadn't divulged she even had Ellie. If Molly had, her pay would have increased. Of that, she was positive.

Carrie Anne laughed. "That sounds like Josiah."

Caroline nodded. "It really does. That boy…Bear is stubborn; Wyatt is wild and spontaneous—"

"That's the truth," Gabby added, laughing.

"Hunter is driven, and Josiah is quirky." His mom took a deep breath. "Yes, we'll go with quirky."

Carrie Anne rolled her eyes. "You mean weird."

Without thinking, Molly said, "He doesn't like that. Being called weird. It hurts his feelings."

"What?" Carrie Anne asked, her eyebrows drawn together.

"You hurt his feelings. I don't think you saw it, but he frowned the other night when you called him weird." Molly held Carrie Anne's gaze.

Carrie Anne's forehead furrowed. "I wasn't trying to. Weird isn't bad. It's just…weird."

Gabby bumped her shoulder against Carrie Anne's. "Yeah, but he's always been sensitive." She looked at

Molly. "He's got a big heart. He's easy-going and simple."

Nodding, Reagan said, "I have to agree with that. Josiah, Hunter, Bear, Wyatt…all four are good men."

Carrie Anne returned Gabby's shoulder bump. "And you chose the craziest West of them all."

"You mean I chose two of the craziest," Gabby said and burst out cackling.

"Shut up." Carrie Anne poked Gabby in the side.

Reagan snickered. "They always bicker like this."

"We do not," Carrie Anne and Gabby said at the same time.

Pauline sighed. "Girls, we are in public. Act your age."

Stephanie snorted. "They are."

"Shut up," Carrie Anne and Gabby said at the same time.

Caroline gave the two girls a look, and they settled down. "Molly is going to run away if you three keep it up." She grinned. "Just so you know, it's pretty much like this all the time with this family."

"I love it," Molly said, and she did. If she had to pick a family to join, it would be this one.

Carrie Anne leveled her eyes at Molly. "Join us."

"Uh-oh." Reagan shook her head and looked down. "There she goes."

"What?" asked Molly, glancing from Reagan to Carrie Anne.

"Josiah likes you. You can see it in the way he looks at you," Carrie Anne said, seeming to ignore Reagan.

Gabby rolled her eyes. "Carrie Anne is the resident matchmaker. One of these days, she's going to retire from teaching and open up her own business."

"Hush." Carrie Anne side-eyed Gabby. "I'm right about this. Josiah likes you."

As sweet as that sounded, Molly couldn't entertain that kind of thought. "I made a rule when I adopted Ellie that I wouldn't date. I love my mom, but the continual dating was hard on me and my brother. I don't want that for Ellie."

Carrie Anne nodded, but Molly got the distinct impression Josiah's sister wanted to press it. "I respect you for that. It couldn't have been an easy decision to adopt. Is it finalized?"

"Not quite, but it will be soon. It's just a matter of paperwork at this point." If Molly remembered correctly, Derek and Brenda would've received their notice of rights termination. Once that was done, the last thing was the judge signing off on it.

"Okay, just one last thing. It would be awesome if Travis and Ellie grew up together. So, even if you don't want to date Josiah, you still have to visit a lot." Carrie Anne smiled wide.

Molly snickered. "I've wandered into a Borg hive, and resistance is futile?"

Josiah's sister tilted her head and gave her a puzzled look. "Uh, what?"

"Oh, nothing." Josiah would have gotten the joke. They spoke each other's language. Something Molly never thought she'd find in a guy who wasn't still living in their parent's basement.

"It sounds like something Josiah would get, though. Am I right?" Carrie Anne asked Molly.

Nodding, Molly's cheeks heated. Her head was saying she wouldn't break her rule, but her heart was not listening to reason at all. She liked Josiah. More than liked, she was falling for him. It certainly wasn't hard. A gorgeous, goofy guy who was kind and generous. What more could a woman ask for?

Nothing. When it came to Josiah, Molly's opinion was that he was the Danny Phantom to her Sam. Square pegs in a world of round holes. And she liked it. She liked it a lot.

∽

BLACK FRIDAY SHOPPING took all day. By the time

Molly shuffled into the house that evening, she was exhausted. She'd been anxious to get back and see Ellie, so Josiah's family offered to put her things away.

Josiah met her at the bottom of the stairs, holding Ellie. He lifted her a little and smiled. "And this, Ellie, is why we don't go Black Friday shopping." He laughed.

Molly blew out a big breath and sagged. "I've never done that before. It was wild." She held up her hand. "But I got a baby monitor and a pack-n-play for a steal. I even got you a gift." She rolled her lips in, trying to hide her Cheshire grin.

"What?"

"You heard me." She waggled her finger at him. "There was too much money in that envelope, mister."

He tilted his head, and his lips quirked up. "You had fun, though, didn't you?"

Nodding, she said, "Yeah, but I do feel guilty."

"Don't." He lowered his gaze. "I like making you smile. You work hard and take care of a baby. Having a treat every now and again is okay."

She walked to him and hugged him with one arm as she tickled Ellie's neck. "Thank you. I've said it, but it really doesn't adequately express my gratitude."

Josiah pressed a kiss to the top of her head. "You have. Trust me."

She lifted a little on her toes and kissed his cheek. "I had so much fun today. You've watched her all day. I think it's my turn."

"Why don't you go take a bath? I'll feed and change her and then bring her to you when you're done. You can't convince me you don't need to wash off all that shopping."

As much as she wanted to argue with him, she couldn't. "Okay."

"I promise I'll bring her to you. She needs her momma as much as you need her." He smiled.

They locked eyes, and Molly combed her fingers through his hair. Heartbeat after heartbeat, they just stood there.

She was falling for him. It wasn't even a question anymore. She was falling for the "weird," sensitive, sweet, funny guy who cared about people and treated her like no one ever had.

Just as she went to kiss him, his phone rang, and he fished it out of his pocket. "Oh man," he said and looked at her. "I have to take this. It's for work."

"This late? On the Friday after Thanksgiving?"

He nodded. "I'm sorry." He handed Ellie to Molly. "I'll make it up to you later. I promise." He put the phone to his ear, walked around her, and rushed out of the living room and down the hall.

For a second, she was upset that he'd rushed off, but he'd taken care of Ellie all day. Just because she couldn't take a bath right that second didn't mean he'd always put work first.

Plus, it wasn't like she could command all his time. Sure, they'd grown closer, but he'd seemed to respect her decisions. Not once had he pushed her to change her mind. Although, with the way her thoughts were going, he didn't need to push. They were shifting on their own.

She closed her eyes and took a deep breath. It was too much, too soon to even be thinking about any of this stuff. Ellie was more than enough for Molly. Besides, she didn't need a guy to ride in like Prince Charming and save the day. She could fight her battles on her own.

CHAPTER 9

The sun had just hit the horizon on its way into the sky as Josiah shuffled into the kitchen. He grabbed a cup and poured himself some coffee before taking a seat at the bar. Yawning, he rubbed his face, trying to wake himself up. It had been a week since Thanksgiving, and he and Molly were taking turns getting up with Ellie during the night. They'd played rock, paper, scissors, lizards, Spock to see if they'd share the responsibility, and he'd won.

It had been Molly's turn that night, but that hadn't kept him from hearing Ellie's cries. He wasn't upset about it, more amused than anything. In no time at all, he'd gone from being able to sleep through an earthquake to hearing the tiny cries of a baby who…he almost thought *didn't belong to him*, but she did.

Maybe not in the legal sense, but there was an Ellie-shaped spot in his heart. He loved her. Innocent, sweet, and able to wrap grown men around her finger with a single smile. She was Super Ellie, and he absolutely, whole-heartedly loved that little girl. In the last week, he'd found himself reevaluating his goals. Realtor of the Year was important, but Ellie…Dad of the Year had moved up several spots on his list since meeting her.

As he took a sip of his coffee, his sister walked into the kitchen. "Rough night?"

"No, it was Molly's turn last night, but it's hard to turn off hearing Ellie." He raked his hand through his hair, trying to push a few of the strands from his face. Add to that staying up late to get the tree up and decorated, and it had made for a long, long night.

She poured herself a cup of coffee and sat on the stool next to Josiah's. Together they took a sip and sighed. "This has to be the best coffee ever brewed," she said.

He nodded. "I crave it nightly."

"What?" She looked at him funny.

"*So I Married An Axe Murderer*. Mike Meyers?"

She shook her head. "No clue."

Shrugging, he said, "It was suggested after I watched this other movie. It was awesome."

"If you say so." She bumped him with her shoulder. "Molly speaks your language too. She said something about burgers and fertility."

Burgers and fertility? What kind of discussion were they having? Then it hit him. "The Borg? Resistance is futile?"

She swallowed the sip of coffee she'd just taken. "That's it. I had no idea what she was talking about."

"How did your brain turn that into burgers and fertility?" He laughed.

"My brain? The better question is, how did you get Borg and resistance is futile out of burgers and fertility?"

They quietly drank their coffee for a few minutes before Carrie Anne set her cup down. "She likes you, you know."

How did he know that was coming? "You put me on a dating website, and I will never speak to you again."

Carrie Anne scoffed and feigned being mortally wounded. "I was being a wonderful, loving sister by putting Bear on that website. And it's been, like, what? Two years now. Let it go."

"I haven't watched that movie." He grinned, and his heart said, *Yet.* If Ellie wanted to watch *Frozen*, he'd be right there with her, Milk-Duds popcorn and Twizzlers as well.

"Whatever. I'm right, though. She likes you, and you like her." She leveled her eyes at him. "You're perfect for each other, and you know it."

Shaking his head, he engulfed the rest of his coffee before standing. "That might be, but she doesn't want to date, and I'm not going to push it. Besides, I can't think about that right now. I have my own reasons for not dating at the moment."

Carrie Anne stood and grabbed his arm. "Wait. I actually wanted to talk to you about something else."

He set his mug on the kitchen island counter, expecting her to ask why he couldn't date. "What?"

"Molly mentioned something during lunch while we were shopping last week, and it's been bugging me ever since."

Slowly, he took his seat again, and so did Carrie Anne.

"She said when I call you weird it hurts your feelings."

"Uh…" Molly told her that? Definitely not what he expected.

"I had no idea. I meant it as a good thing, but I guess to you, it felt like I was making fun of you. I promise I wasn't. I like that you do things differently.

You're a great person. I love you to pieces, and I wish I'd known all this time that I'd been hurting you." Her eyes turned glassy. "I'm so sorry."

Whoa. He'd always just tried to let it roll off his back. It had hurt for a second, but he knew she wasn't trying to be mean. All of his siblings ribbed him, so it wasn't like she was the only one. "It's okay. I know you weren't."

"No, it's not okay. I'm really sorry for hurting you. I'll try to be conscious of it from now on."

He hugged her and smiled. "Thanks."

When he lifted his gaze, Molly was standing in the doorway, chewing her lip. He mouthed, *Thank you.*

She winked and stepped back, deliberately making a noise as she reentered. "Good morning. Ellie's asleep, so I'm grabbing a quick cup of coffee."

Carrie Anne quickly wiped her eyes and walked to the door. "Uh, I'm going to get ready for the day. I'll see you guys in a while."

Josiah waited until she was out of earshot before asking, "How did you know being called weird bothered me?"

"Your lips turned down when she said it. We were having lunch in the middle of all that shopping, and I mentioned it." She filled her mug with coffee, took a sip, and wilted. "I might have to figure out a way to have this shipped to me."

She approached him and set her cup down. "You've been so good to me. I think I'd fight off a bear for you."

He narrowed his eyes. "Grizzly or black?"

"Sugar-free gummy." She giggled.

"That's a serious bear. Have you read the reviews?"

She covered her mouth with her hand as she leaned on the counter, laughing. "Yes. They're hysterical."

He was laughing as hard as she was. Then he began telling her that his sister couldn't remember the Borg. By the time he was done, his stomach was hurting from the laughing.

"Fertility? Really?"

He drew a cross over his heart. "I promise. At first, I was like, what exactly were you talking about? Then it hit me. Oh man."

"Stop, stop, stop," she said and groaned. "Oh, my sides." She took a deep breath and stretched. "I haven't laughed like that in I don't know how long."

"Me either." He yawned.

"Did you not sleep well?" she asked.

How could he tell her without making her feel guilty? Short answer: he didn't. "Um…I slept okay."

She crossed her arms over her chest. "That's not

true." Stepping into him, she palmed the side of his face and ran her thumb across his cheek. "What was wrong?"

"I think I'm programmed to wake up with Ellie."

Her jaw dropped.

Shaking his head, he covered her hand with his. "No, it's okay. I hope this doesn't make things weird, but…I love her. I'd get up with her a hundred times a night."

Her lips parted just slightly, and she whispered, "Josiah…"

He dropped his hand and lowered his gaze. "I shouldn't have said anything. I'm sorry." He felt hollowed-out. He could already hear the pulling away.

"Yes, you should have." She lifted on her toes and kissed his forehead. "You are without a doubt the most special man I've ever met. Ellie is a lucky little girl to have you in her corner."

Lifting his gaze to hers, he smiled, relief filling him. But it wasn't lost on him that she'd called him special. He'd heard those words before, and they were used for guys who'd been permanently friend-zoned. He already knew that's where she'd put him, but that word was the nail in the coffin.

Even if she did like him, which he suspected Carrie Anne was just being her typical matchmaker self, it didn't mean she thought of him as more than a friend. It wasn't just her either. Ellie was in the equation. He needed to keep his distance if for no other reason than he didn't want to jeopardize his friendship with Molly.

Friends wasn't great, but he could live with it. What he couldn't do is live without either Molly or Ellie. That little girl was a done deal, and her mom wasn't far behind. In his mind, a woman who could play rock, paper, scissors, lizard, Spock was a keeper.

His heart hiccupped. He was falling for Molly. The one perfect girl for him. She didn't want to date, and he couldn't date. His timing was about as good as his ability to pick food delivery. Horrible.

∽

WITH ONE LAST MIRROR CHECK, Molly walked out of the bathroom. Taking turns getting up with Ellie had done wonders for Molly. She felt more refreshed and put-together than she ever had. When she and Josiah played rock, paper, scissors, lizard, Spock, she was sure he cheated somehow.

As she reached the door to his room, she softly leaned against the frame, watching him with Ellie. He was in the middle of the bed, propped on his elbows, kissing her cheeks and talking to her. It was so sweet.

Ellie batted at his nose and then held the tip of it.

"Yeah, that's my nose. You have one too," he said and touched the tip of her nose with his finger.

She babbled, and he chuckled. "Baby translator activated. You got it right. Nose." He kissed one cheek. "You." He kissed the other. "Are." He kissed her forehead. "So stinking adorable." He smothered her with kisses all around her face.

As Molly stood there, it took no effort at all to see him next to her. When she'd called him special, she'd meant it. Somehow, this incredible man had followed her out of a coffee shop, given her a job, and invited her into his life—a life with a family she'd only ever dreamed of belonging to.

On top of all that, he *loved* Ellie. As horrible as he was with a poker face, it hadn't been a shocking revelation. What man would get up with a baby if he didn't have some connection with her?

It was scary; she couldn't deny that. What if he got angry with Molly and decided he was done? She couldn't picture him actually doing that, but as a kid, she'd learned that just because she couldn't see it happening didn't mean it wouldn't.

Josiah turned his attention to Molly and smiled. "Hey. You look great."

"Yeah, because runway fashion is a faded Metallica t-shirt and jeans."

"I've seen the runway. I prefer your look."

She walked to the bed and sat beside him, putting her finger in Ellie's hand. "Hi, Ellie."

Ellie rolled her head and cooed at Molly.

"Hey, you two," Caroline said as she came into Josiah's room.

"Hi…Caroline." Molly wasn't comfortable calling her that yet. It felt odd, but Josiah's mom had insisted on being called by her first name.

Josiah rolled to his side and faced his mom. "What's up?"

"Carrie Anne, Reagan, and I are going down to the orchard. Gabby's been working on an apple-pecan pie recipe. Next weekend is their monthly farmer's market, and she wants us to test it. Your dad is out with Bear and Hunter. I called him, and he said they'd meet us there. You three are more than welcome to join us."

"Pie?" Molly was in like Flynn. The three words she loved most were *I've got pie*. Unlike most women, her dream proposal was: *I love you, and I have pie*. "I love pie."

Caroline brightened. "Great. I'm sure Gabby would love your opinion. She'd probably thinks the rest of us are just being nice."

Josiah used his feet to grab a diaper at the end of the bed and began changing Ellie. "Okay, we'll see you guys in a little bit."

As soon as Caroline left, Molly turned to him. "I think I'll change shirts. It won't take me but a second."

He smiled. "Take your time. Knowing Gabby, there's enough pie to feed an army."

"Yeah, well, when it comes to pie, I'm all four branches of the military, including the Coast Guard."

Laughing, Josiah shook his head. "Okay, I'll have Ellie ready and packed by the time you change."

"Awesome," she said, briskly walking to the door and pausing as she reached it. "I've already said it a million times, but thank you for inviting us."

He looked up and smiled. "I'm glad you came."

With a small nod, she walked to her room and shut the door, leaning back against it. It was wonderful that he'd invited her, but at the same time, she could so get used to all of it. Now she had to figure out how to enjoy herself and remember that this was her glass-slipper night. Only, she'd end up barefoot because a prince just wasn't in her future.

Yes, she liked Josiah. It was beyond great that he loved Ellie, but a relationship…she couldn't go around breaking the rules she set for herself—even if the small voice in the back of her head said otherwise.

Only, the voice wasn't so small anymore. It had gotten its hands on a megaphone, and it was so loud her ears were ringing. Why did things have to be so confusing all the time?

CHAPTER 10

On the drive to the orchard, Josiah had finally remembered to give Molly the promised rundown on what Carrie Anne had tried to do to his brother Bear. She'd been just as shocked as everyone else that his sister had tried to put his brother on a dating website. The whole family had wondered what Carrie Anne was thinking. Two years later, Bear was still a little sore on that subject.

"I guess I didn't realize how big this place was. Just how big is this ranch?" asked Molly as they pulled into the drive and parked.

"Uh, over nine hundred acres."

Her eyes widened. "Whoa. That's a lot of acres. I definitely didn't know it was that huge."

He laughed. "Yeah, Bear has always loved this place.

When we were kids, he'd tell us all the things he'd do if he ever had the chance to own it." He twisted in the seat, took Ellie from the car seat, and cradled her.

Man, he loved this baby. It was the scariest thing he'd ever realized. It would absolutely break his heart if he didn't have her in his life. He kissed her cheek and smiled at her. Then he realized it was super quiet. When he looked up, Molly was staring at him.

"What?" he asked.

A smile slowly spread on her lips. "Nothing. Just… you're really good with her."

"I think you'd have to work at being bad with a baby." He chuckled. "Plus," he said, turning Ellie to Molly, "who can resist this little face?"

Wrinkling her nose, Molly nodded. "You have a point." She turned and fetched the diaper bag in the back seat. "May as well take this in. There's pie, and I have a feeling this might take a while."

"At least I know what to get you for Christmas." He shot her a cheesy grin.

"This is true. You get me pie, and we are square." She laughed.

Josiah opened his door, stepped out, and met Molly on the other side. Together, they walked to the front door and knocked.

The door opened, and Wyatt was laughing. "Hey,

Josiah." His brother stepped aside, allowing them to enter. "Come on in. Make yourselves at home."

"Hey, Wyatt," Josiah said.

Gabby crossed the room and stopped beside Wyatt. "Hey, guys."

"Hey, thanks for inviting us to have pie," Molly said as she slipped out of her coat and hung it up.

All Josiah heard was *us*, and he loved how it sounded. If only it could happen. It couldn't and wouldn't, though, and he needed to remember that. His heart was going to get broken if he didn't watch it.

"Of course," Gabby said and smiled. "The more taste testers I have, the better."

Wyatt and Gabby returned to the living room, leaving Josiah and Molly by the door. Josiah turned to her. "I'm guessing you don't get much girl time at home, so if you want, I'll take care of Ellie so you can spend some time with the women."

Molly stared at him and then mumbled something under her breath he couldn't make out. She inhaled deeply, and her lips quirked up. "Thank you. Actually, I could really use that."

He was beginning to love how he was the source of some of her smiles. "Okay, well, I've got her. Eat some pie, gab with Gabby." He winked.

Lifting on her toes, Molly placed a kiss on his cheek. "Thank you."

"You bet," Josiah replied and watched Molly nearly float over to the women who were talking. He lowered his gaze to Ellie. "I think your mommy needed some serious adult conversation. How about me and you find a recliner and nap? What do you say?"

Ellie gurgled and cooed, wiggling a little as she did.

"I have all sorts of great ideas, don't I?"

She wrapped her hand around his finger. Oh man, he was done for. This little girl had his heart, but that was okay.

His phone rang, and he pulled it from his pocket. It was his client Malakai Raven, the lead singer of Crush…again. He'd been the one who'd called so late on Black Friday.

Josiah sandwiched the phone between his shoulder and his ear. "Hello?"

"Hey, I looked through those properties you sent me, but I don't think any of them would be great for a restaurant location. I really need that eclectic rocker vibe, you know?"

No, Josiah didn't know, not really. But the sites he'd shown Malakai did give him an idea of what to avoid. "Well, when I get back to Dallas in January, I could look again now that I know what you don't like."

"Well, that's the problem. We've been asked to perform live in Times Square New Year's Eve, and then we're going on tour. I need to find the location so my partner, Tyler, can get to work."

"Uh, okay," Josiah said and looked around the room. "Hold on one second."

"Sure."

Muting the phone, Josiah walked over to Molly. "Hey, I'm so sorry, but I have to take this. It's…"

Molly took Ellie. "What's going on?"

His mom looked up at him from where she was sitting. "Are you leaving?"

Nodding, he said, "Yeah, I have some work I need to take care of."

"Work? We barely see you. Can't it wait until after the holidays?" his mom asked.

"No, I can't put it off."

Molly held his gaze a moment. "Will you be back soon?"

He shrugged. "Uh, I don't know. I'm not sure how long this will take. If I don't get back before you're ready to leave…" He looked at his mom. "Could you give her a ride home if I'm not back before you guys head back to the house?"

"Sure," his mom replied.

"I'm okay with that." That's what Molly's lips said,

but the look she was giving him said it was anything but okay.

His shoulders sagged. "If I could, I'd tell you more, but I can't. I signed a confidentiality agreement."

"We're good." This time Molly gave him a real smile, or at least it looked like a real smile.

"I'll get the car seat and leave it before I go." Josiah leaned down and kissed Ellie. "This is the last time, I promise. I'll see you later."

He strode to the front door, grabbed his coat, and slipped outside, taking his phone off mute. "Hey, Malakai, sorry to keep you waiting."

More than anything, Josiah was sorry for leaving. For the longest time, his mind had been set on becoming Realtor of the Year, and now he wondered if maybe it wasn't what he wanted. It sure didn't make him feel successful. Not when he had to leave the two girls he cared about most.

Shaking his head, he cleared his thoughts. Just a few weeks. That's all he needed. Then he could think about other goals. Goals like love and family and kids.

∼

MOLLY CUT through her slice of pie and took a bite. Good heavens, it was delicious. With the way the kitchen smelled of cinnamon and nutmeg and apples, there was no way it was going to taste bad. Gabby had used fresh pecans, roasted pecans, and several other varieties including everything from maple-baked to honey-toasted pecans.

Groaning, Molly closed her eyes, absolutely certain she'd died and gone to pie heaven. "Oh, girl, this is so good."

"You've said that about all of them." Gabby laughed.

"Because it's true. They're so good. I think my favorite is that one." Molly pointed to the maple-roasted-pecan apple pie with the laced crust topping. "There's something about that maple that just melts in your mouth."

Gabby nodded. "That's my favorite too. Wyatt says it's too sweet for him."

Molly absolutely loved Gabby. Well, she loved all of them. They were as genuine now as they'd been when they'd gone shopping. They weren't putting on fronts or being nice. They were all just good people. They didn't think she was weird for loving comic books and *Sharknado*. If only Josiah had been there to back her up about it being a great movie.

When he'd left her on the night of Black Friday, she'd waved it off. Today, though, it hit her harder. It wasn't just her he'd let down; it was his family too.

The people he said he loved. If he could leave them, did she even stand a chance? Not just her, but Ellie too. Could Ellie count on him to be there when she was in a play? What if he promised to be there and didn't show up?

Carrie Anne walked into the kitchen and took a seat next to Molly. Leaning forward with her arms on the table, she sighed. "It's a really good thing you weren't doing this pie stuff before I got married. My dress wouldn't have fit."

"I'm thinking I should've packed my set of Thanksgiving pants," Molly added. "I'm gonna be waddling by the time I get back to Dallas."

Josiah's sister smiled, and her eyes narrowed a fraction.

"No, Carrie Anne!" Gabby popped her on the arm. "Don't even think about it."

She scoffed. "What? All I did was smile."

Gabby leveled her eyes at Carrie Anne and pointed a finger at her. "I know you, remember?"

Molly lifted an eyebrow. "Do I want to know what that was all about?"

Sighing, Gabby said, "That look is the one that gets you put on a dating website or pretending to date a guy to make someone else jealous."

"In my defense, the last one worked." Carrie Anne

crossed her arms over her chest as she sat back. "And as for the first, Bear is just difficult. He didn't even give it a chance."

Molly sucked in a sharp breath. "You were gonna matchmake me?"

"Yes," Gabby said.

At the same time, Carrie Anne replied, "No."

Pointing at Gabby, Molly chuckled. "I think I believe her."

Carrie Anne's lips quirked up. "I was just thinking…you fit here, and wouldn't it be awesome if we were sisters. That's all. I know you said you don't date, but…well, I think you and Josiah would be great together."

"That's sweet, but I can't break my rule. Before I adopted Ellie, I made that promise." The longer she was around him, the dumber her rule became. He wasn't the kind of guy to cut and run if things got difficult. She knew it in her heart, but her head was putting up a defense that could rival a seasoned lawyer. "Most guys don't want to date a single mom. I figured it would just be easier that way."

"Clearly, Josiah doesn't have that problem," Carrie Anne said.

Molly took another bite of pie, trying to think of a reasonable argument. Her problem was, she didn't have any. Josiah was amazing, even if he had left her for work again. It was the second time, but they weren't dating. Maybe things would be different if they were.

"I will admit that." She held up her finger. "But, that doesn't change the rule. It's not just about whether he gets along with Ellie or even loves her. Two people can love a child and have it still not work out between them." That was the part that scared her the most. Falling in love with him and it not working out. Not just for the safety of her own heart, but his as well. "I lived it. I don't want that for Ellie."

Carrie Anne leaned back. "You have a point."

"I can't fault you either," Gabby added. "Having Travis made things so different. I've known and loved Wyatt since I can remember, but once I held this tiny little human, my whole world view shifted. I love Wyatt and would do anything for him. But Travis? I'd move heaven and earth for him. It's a love I had no idea I was capable of having."

Carrie Anne grinned. "I don't know how it is to hold my own child in my hands…yet."

Gabby gasped. "Really?"

Josiah's sister nodded. "I took the pregnancy test last night. I had to tell someone, but I want to see the doctor before telling the whole family."

A loud inhale caught their attention, and they turned. Josiah's mom was standing in the doorway with her hand to her mouth, eyes wide and tearful. "You're pregnant?"

Carrie Anne stood. "Yeah. At least, that's what the test said."

Her mom rushed forward and hugged her. "Ohhh, honey. This is the best news since Gabby's last Christmas."

Molly wished she'd had this kind of reaction to adopting Ellie. Her shoulders rounded, and she cast her gaze to the table as she remembered Ellie's birth. It was supposed to be a happy day—a day of joy—but her mom had tried to hide a scowl. The nurses had tried to hand Ellie to Brenda when she was delivered, but she'd refused. Then they'd handed her to Derek, who promptly handed her to Molly.

The next thing Molly knew, her thoughts were being interrupted by an arm going across her shoulders, and Caroline was taking a seat next to her. "Sweetheart, we are thrilled you brought Ellie, and I would love to be her grandma, if you'll let me. In my opinion, I can't have too many grandbabies, and she fits just fine here."

Oh, Molly felt awful for stealing Carrie Anne's

moment. "I'm so sorry. I didn't mean to take away from Carrie Anne."

Carrie Anne joined her mom and stood next to her. "You didn't. Everything's fine. Besides, I really don't want anything big until there's a doctor telling me I'm pregnant."

Caroline squeezed Molly's shoulders tighter. "Honey, we're family. You'd be hard-pressed to get any of us riled up. The only thing I'd be upset with is you not coming to family holidays or even a few trips in between. That little girl of yours is precious. I love her to pieces."

Blinking back tears, Molly nodded, and Caroline hugged her. "I don't know when you decided you were in the way or a burden, but you're not, sweetheart. It takes special people to adopt, and you are pretty special in my opinion."

She'd known these people all of a week, and they'd completely rocked her world. If nothing else, she wanted to protect her friendship with Josiah just so she could let Ellie grow up with people who appreciated the life they were given.

Molly's mom was good to her, loved her and Derek, but not once had she ever made her feel wanted. Not like this. Molly wanted Ellie to have *this*. A place and people to turn to when the world was cold, unmerciful, and mean. The kind of people who would hold her and love her and show her how to go out into the world and do the same.

Agreeing to come home with Josiah was one of the smartest decisions she'd ever made, other than adopting Ellie. She'd never be able to repay him, but she'd sure try to find a way.

CHAPTER 11

Sitting in her room, Molly rocked Ellie as she looked out the window. It had been a few days since the pie tasting. The days were filled with walks, playing cards, and literally becoming addicted to Reagan West's coffee. She'd been half-heartedly kidding when she'd talked about having it shipped in. Now, she wasn't kidding at all.

The time had also given her a chance to think even more about her own childhood. When she was a kid, the holidays were okay. When her mom wasn't dating someone, sometimes she'd be home for Thanksgiving and Christmas. Other times she'd be at work. The holidays weren't anything special, and they didn't have extended family to visit.

Her phone rang, and she quickly grabbed it out of

her pocket before it woke Ellie. "Hello?" she answered without checking the caller ID.

"Hey, sweetheart." It was her mom with the obligatory Happy Thanksgiving. Well, belated. Each year it was different. Sometimes, her mom would call on the holiday. Others, she'd either call later or forget altogether.

"Hey, Mom. Happy Thanksgiving."

"We were in town and stopped by your apartment. You haven't moved, have you?"

Molly grunted a laugh. "No, I was invited to spend the holidays with a friend."

"A friend?" The slight rise in her mom's voice wasn't missed.

"Just a friend."

"I was hoping to see Ellie."

"I'm sorry, Mom. I didn't know. Usually, you and Dad are out of town, visiting his family."

"Well, I know, but this year is different. You have my granddaughter." She took a deep breath. "I'm still a little shocked that neither you nor your brother thought to ask me if I wanted her. I've been a single mom, and I know how hard it is. I didn't want that for you."

Molly stood and walked to the crib to lay Ellie

down. "Mom, I'm doing fine. I love her, and she's well taken care of."

"On a housekeeper's wage? I don't see how that's possible. And your apartment is too small to raise a child."

It was the same argument made before Brenda made her choice. Her mom had a stable income, a home, and the baby would have two parents. It made more sense for her to adopt Ellie, not Molly.

Ultimately, it was up to Brenda, and she'd chosen Molly. Her mom hadn't liked it at the time, but it was better that Ellie stayed with family. That way, they knew she was being taken care of.

Since then, nothing had been said. Her mom had even been at the hospital when Ellie was born and visited the week after she was home. Until now, Molly thought it was settled.

"We've had this conversation. I wanted her. Things may not be perfect, but I love my life with Ellie."

Her mom cleared her throat. "Derek and Brenda received the paperwork notifying them that their rights were being severed about a week ago. We've talked some more, and they agree with us that your dad and I should have her."

Molly's heart rate doubled. "What does that mean? I'm her mother. You can't just take her from me."

"I was hoping the two of us could talk and make this as easy for both you and Ellie as we can. That we could come to an agreement."

Sucking in a lungful of air, Molly tried to make sense of what she was hearing. "Brenda wanted me to have her. The adoption is one step away from done. You can't do this."

"Actually, we've talked to a lawyer. Since the adoption isn't finalized yet, Derek and Brenda can switch custody from you to us. The lawyer says that if we can show we're a better fit, we'll have a good shot at being granted custody." She paused. "That's not how I want to handle it, but she's my granddaughter, and I want what's best for her."

Easing herself down on the corner of the bed, Molly's entire body was shaking. Her mom was talking about ripping her daughter away from her. "I'm what's best for her."

"Molly, I love you, and I think you are a fantastic person, but you really aren't in any shape to take on the responsibility of a baby."

Molly wanted to pinch herself. This had to be a nightmare. "I'm twenty-nine years old, twelve years older than you when you had Derek, and apparently, you were just fine being a single parent."

Her mom took a deep breath. "This is different."

"Is this why you were stopping by my apartment? To discuss stealing my child from me? How much money did you offer them?" That's the only thing Molly could think of that would have made Derek and Brenda change their minds.

Her mom scoffed. "We didn't offer them anything, and we're not stealing her from you." She sighed heavily. "You deserve a life that's not weighed down with a child. You're young. There's plenty of time to have children when you're older."

Molly stood. "Ellie is not a weight. She is the best thing to ever happen to me, and I love her. She's my little girl, and you can't have her." She clicked the end button, and her lips trembled as hot tears ran down her cheeks.

A knock came from her door. "Molly, it's Josiah."

Normally, she hated for someone to catch her crying, but she wasn't sure she'd ever stop at this point. She walked to the door and opened it.

Josiah sucked in a sharp breath. "What's wrong?"

She stepped into him as the tears fell harder, and he put his arms around her, setting his cheek on top of her head. "I'm here. Whatever it is, you can count on me." He squeezed her tighter, and it felt like he was the only thing holding her together.

Leaning back, she sniffled and hiccupped. "My

mom is trying to take Ellie from me."

"Why?" His eyebrows furrowed. "You're a great mom."

"Derek and Brenda have changed their minds about who they want to have custody. My mom has talked to a lawyer, and since the adoption isn't finalized, they can challenge it." She dissolved into tears again and balled her fists in his t-shirt. "They're going to take her."

He held her out from him. "She's not taking Ellie from you."

It was so sweet that he was saying it, but he couldn't be sure of that. Derek and Brenda were Ellie's parents. The adoption wasn't final, and they could change their minds. Plus, Molly didn't have the finances to fight them. Josiah paid her well, but her parents had deeper pockets. If Brenda and her brother had changed their minds, there was nothing she could do. She didn't even know where they were or if they were even together anymore.

"That's really sweet of you, but knowing my mom, she wouldn't have said anything if she didn't think there was a possibility of it happening." She turned and pulled away from him, stopping at the end of the crib to watch Ellie sleep. "She'd said something before I began the adoption process, but I had no idea she was still thinking about it. I honestly thought it was settled. I don't have the money to fight it."

"I do," Josiah said.

She looked at him. He was a good man, and she appreciated his offer. "I—"

"Molly, I'm a billionaire."

She barked a tiny laugh. "I know you're trying to make me feel better, but I just need a second to figure out what I'm going to do."

He crossed the room and stopped in front of her. "No, Molly, I'm a billionaire. Do you remember a few years ago, that lottery that rolled over forever? The one that was so big that people were buying hundreds of tickets at a time?"

Now that he said it, she did. She'd even purchased a ticket. Of course, she'd known it was a waste of a dollar, but it had been fun to dream. "Yeah."

"My brothers and sister and I won it. That's how Bear bought this ranch. We won that lottery. I'm a billionaire."

Her eyes widened. "Wow."

"That's what I thought." He chuckled nervously. "I'm still not used to it. Nothing about me has changed. I've invested some of it and given some away, but for the most part, it's just sitting there."

Based on his truck, she believed it. It wasn't new,

and if he'd been changed by money, the truck would have been the first thing to upgrade. He was a Texan, after all. "You're the anonymous person who paid all those medical debts off, aren't you? The one in the story who was all over the news and social media?"

A tiny grin spread on his lips, and he shrugged. "Yeah."

As much as she appreciated his offer, she couldn't take his money. It wouldn't be right. "Still, this isn't your problem. I need to take care of this."

"That's where you're wrong. You're my friend. Your problems are my problems." He crossed his arms over his chest. "Your mom is not taking Ellie." There was a determination in his voice…and it was kind of cool. The normally happy, easy-going guy was in *Mortal Kombat* mode.

Molly placed her hand on his forearm. "I don't want you to think I'm taking advantage of you. What you've done already is more than I could have ever dreamed of. I've loved being here."

His arms dropped to his sides. "You aren't. I'm offering, and I'm telling you, Ellie is staying right where she belongs. With you. I have a friend who is a lawyer. He'll point me to the right person."

Molly hugged him around the chest. "I don't know how to say thank you."

"I like hugs," he said as he wrapped his arms around her and kissed the top of her head. "So this works."

The hug continued, and the longer he held her, the more she wanted to stay right where she was. Closing her eyes, she inhaled, drinking him in and reveling in his comfort. For the tiniest moment, she could picture them standing just like this while they watched their children playing in the backyard.

Leaning back, she lifted her gaze to his, and the battle between her head and her heart hit an all-time high. She wasn't going to date. It was a promise, a sacrifice she was willing to make for Ellie, but...her stomach twisted in a knot as the battle reached a new intensity.

She palmed his cheek, and her gaze drifted to his lips. She'd never wanted to kiss someone as much as she wanted to kiss him.

Josiah covered her hand with his and touched his lips to hers. She slid her hand along his jaw and rested it on the back of his neck, drawing closer and soaking up his warmth. The soft kiss continued, and she couldn't get enough.

As she circled her arms around his neck, his arms tightened around her. She'd always wondered what a foot-pop kiss felt like, and this had to be it. The kind that melted her brain, turned her inside out, and made her forget that problems existed. It was the kind of kiss that made her rethink everything.

He broke the kiss, and she held his gaze. She had no idea what he was thinking. For that matter, she didn't know what she was thinking. Well, other than she liked it. A sweet kiss from an equally sweet guy.

"Look, I'm—" he began.

Before he could finish the sentence, she cut him off with another longer kiss. The first one was amazing, and this one was even better. Either he was just that great at kissing or she was falling so hard a peck on the lips would have knocked her socks off. It didn't take a lot of thought to decide on the latter of the two. This time when it broke, she smiled sheepishly. "It was a quality control check."

The corners of his lips quirked up. "How'd it go?"

"I don't know yet." She hadn't planned on kissing him, but she could feel the apology coming from him. There didn't need to be one. Not that she wasn't confused, because she was completely confused. She just didn't want to shut down the possibility that it could happen again.

His gaze dipped to the floor, and his cheeks turned the most adorable shade of red. "Is it okay if I thought it was great?"

"It was pretty great." Not just great, fantastic, and she could feel the want for more growing.

"I know you're worried, but I'd come up here to see if you wanted to play cards."

She circled her arms around his neck. "Thank you…for everything," she said and stepped back.

"You're welcome." He took her hand and tangled his fingers in hers. "I *will not* let anyone take Ellie from you, ever." He held her gaze. "I'll go bankrupt before I let that happen. You have my promise on that."

How had she lucked out to find someone like him? Better, who had been watching over her? It had to be more than luck. A guy like Josiah didn't just show up. Not when she needed him the most.

He squeezed her fingers. "When I say I won't let anyone take Ellie, I mean I won't let anyone hurt you either."

More than once, Molly had been let down by people she trusted. And there was a possibility that no matter how hard Josiah fought, they'd still lose, but it was comforting to know she wouldn't be alone.

Silently, she thanked whoever it was looking out for her, for sending Josiah. Not just because he'd help fight for Ellie, but because as much as Molly tried to convince herself she could handle life on her own, it was nice to know she didn't have to.

CHAPTER 12

Finding out that Molly's mom wanted custody of Ellie was a shock to Josiah. Why would she want to do that? She had to know that would not only hurt Molly, but it would hurt their relationship too. Molly was a wonderful mom. Yes, money made things easier, but it certainly didn't love.

Even more shocking were the kisses he and Molly had shared. One second she was looking at him, and the next, he was kissing her. He didn't regret it, but it had been a bold move on his part. Especially knowing she didn't want to date. Granted, kissing and dating were two separate things, but typically, they kind of went hand in hand for most people.

The best part was her kissing him. He'd started to apologize, and *wham*, she was kissing him. She'd called it quality control, which he had to admit was funny. In his mind, it had been the better kiss because she was making the move. Plus, he didn't get the chance to apologize and say he wouldn't do it again. He definitely wanted to kiss her more.

It was Saturday, and that had been a few days ago. Since then, things had felt a little different between them. They had kissed, so it was bound to change things—at least, in his mind.

At the moment, Molly and Josiah had sequestered themselves in Bear's study with the phone on speaker so that if Case had questions, Molly could answer them. Plus, Josiah thought it was only right that she was part of the conversation. He knew if the situation was reversed, he'd want to be included.

"Hey, Josiah, what's up?" Case asked, sounding out of breath. Not unusual as he was training for a half marathon that was coming up soon.

"I was hoping you might be able to point me to a family lawyer."

"Family lawyer? Yeah, I can, but what's up?"

Molly relayed everything to him, and by the time she was done, Josiah could tell Case had stopped running to pay attention.

Ellie began fussing, and without even asking, Molly handed her to Josiah. He gave Molly a cheesy grin, and she wrinkled her nose at him. Since the call with her mom, he'd gone out of his way to try to make her smile or laugh.

"So, if I'm understanding things, the adoption isn't final. They can challenge it." He paused. "Do you believe your mom offered them money?"

Molly crossed her arms over her chest, putting her thumb to her lips and chewing on it. She nodded. "I think so. My brother has been in and out of jail. The last time I cut ties with him was because he stole my credit cards."

Case's breathing had slowed enough that he was no longer panting. "Do you think there are drugs involved?"

"No," Molly said. "He's a thief, but he's not a drug addict, and neither is Brenda. Ellie is a happy, healthy baby girl."

"Okay," Case said. "I think I know someone who can help. She's expensive, but if someone is going to bat for you, you want her."

Josiah nuzzled Ellie with his nose. "If she's the best, then that's who I want."

His friend laughed. "I hope you're really good at real estate."

Molly caught Josiah's gaze and held it, narrowing her eyes. He knew there was a question there, and he'd be answering once the phone call was over.

"I'm great at real estate." He smiled.

"Okay. I'll text you the number and call her to give her a heads-up. These family cases can be time-sensitive."

"Thanks, Case."

They said their goodbyes, and Josiah ended the call.

"He has no idea you have money, does he?" Molly asked. Yep, he'd called it.

"It's not something that comes up. I was being honest when I said I don't feel any different. I'm just me with a lot more zeros." He laughed and then looked down at Ellie. "I love her. I don't doubt your mom wants what's best for her, but she should have offered to help you, not take her."

Sighing, Molly stood. "I think she wants a do-over since she didn't do so well with us. After my dad left my mom, she dated a lot of guys. A lot. Or it felt that way. I wonder if she's always thought the same thing. That she could have done things differently, and maybe my brother wouldn't have been in and out of jail so much."

"But you turned out awesome."

Molly's cheeks turned a soft shade of pink. "Thanks. I just wonder if my mom wants Ellie so she can try again and also as a way to make it up to Derek."

Josiah could understand that. "Did Derek not like your stepdad or something?"

She shook her head. "No, we both love him and refer to him as our dad because he's a good man and always treated us like we belonged to him."

"Yeah?"

She nodded. "After he and my mom were dating for a while, he took my brother and me to dinner. It was a super expensive place where the portions were tiny and the dishes were named things we couldn't pronounce. He asked us if he could marry our mom. No guy had ever done that before. He always included us in everything."

"Sounds like a good guy." Josiah could admire that.

"He picked me up after school one day, and I asked him about it. All the other men my mom dated looked at us like we were just included in the package. But not him. Yes, we came with my mom, but he loved that we were a part of the deal. He said that if he was going to love my mom, he was going to love us too. After that, he was just Dad. He loved us, wholly and unconditionally. Sometimes, it even felt like he loved us more than our mom did."

"Wow. Great guy." Josiah shifted Ellie to his

shoulder and patted her rear. "I think he had the right attitude. I know that's how I'd be." He paused a beat, the statement ringing true because Josiah sure felt like Ellie's dad. If given the opportunity, he'd happily step up to the plate. "You think he's wanting this too?"

"No, I think he's hoping my mom changes her mind once she realizes that it'll hurt me." She hugged herself. "I just feel so blindsided. Derek and Brenda lived with me for four months before she had the baby. Brenda and I talked a lot. The reason she picked me is because she wanted Ellie to have a good life, and money doesn't always equate to good."

Boy, was that true. "No, it doesn't."

"But you and your family are amazing. I kinda think you were the lucky winners of the lottery for a reason." She smiled.

Warmth ran from his stomach to his ears. "I don't know what to say to that."

She walked to him and put her arm around his shoulders, rubbing Ellie's back. "She really likes you."

In an instant, Josiah was seeing his family. Molly, Ellie, and him. A neat little package wrapped in a baby-scented bow. But she already had enough stress on her plate with not just *someone* trying to take her child, but her mom. He'd just met Ellie, and he felt fiercely protective of her, so he could only imagine how Molly felt.

"She's got good taste." He chuckled.

"Josiah, I don't know what I'd do if it weren't for you. I'd have no way to fight this, and I don't know how to repay you."

He slipped his arm around her waist and pulled her tight against him, kissing the top of her head. "We're a team, so you don't have to worry about that." He paused. "Besides, you said you'd fight off a sugar-free gummy bear for me. I'm just saying that's A-game material right there. At this point, it's go big or go home."

Laughing, Molly looked up at him, and in an instant, the air in the room was gone. She touched her lips to his, and the world faded away. If this was another quality control check, it would get a sticker with two thumbs up.

Deepening the kiss, he pulled her closer, loving the feel of her against him. More than anything, he loved the fact that he was holding Ellie and her mom in his arms, knowing they meant the world to him. It felt right to have them there. Like they'd belonged to him before he even knew it.

Slowly, the kiss came to an end, and he touched his forehead to hers.

He'd passed from falling to fallen. These two people were at the center of his sphere. He wanted them both. Maybe with time, Molly would see he wasn't some fair-weather man or part-time wanna-be dad. He wanted this life, and he was willing to be patient and earn it. Molly and Ellie were worth it.

CHAPTER 13

It had taken a couple of days to set up a time to speak to the lawyer Case had referred Molly and Josiah to, Diane Salinas. Apparently, she was in serious demand, and it was for a reason.

Josiah's friend had called her tough, and he wasn't joking. Molly had painstakingly gone over every detail with Diane, starting from the second Derek and Brenda showed up on Molly's doorstep. It was like an interrogation, but Molly understood why.

Then they'd discussed her childhood as well. The lawyer also wanted all the paperwork Molly had filled out and the names of any courthouse employee she'd come in contact with. They'd ended the long, emotionally draining few hours with Diane saying she'd be in touch when she had a chance to review everything.

Since the call, Molly's emotions had been all over the place. One second she was deliriously optimistic, and the next, she was in a ball, crying. She was on rinse and repeat. Get up, worry, and then go to bed and worry even more.

Pushing the covers off, Molly stood and walked to her bedroom door. She needed coffee, and she'd get ready for the day after that. Just as she opened it, Josiah came into view. She startled and jumped, not expecting anyone to be there.

He took her by the arms. "I'm so sorry. I didn't mean to scare you."

She let out a long breath. "It's okay."

Josiah had been nothing but extraordinary. He'd listened to her talk about the same worries over and over without showing even a sign that he was upset or bored. He'd held her more than once while she cried. He was her idea of Superman, offering comfort and care.

Molly stepped into him, and his arms wrapped around her as she laid her head on his chest. "I want to stop being worried. I don't know how you do it," she said, leaning back and locking eyes with him. He seemed so confident all the time.

"I'm worried, but you're her mother. I figure when we win, I'll show a crack in my armor." He smiled. "My job right now is to take care of my two favorite girls in the whole wide world."

"Where is Ellie?"

"My mom has her. That's why I was coming up here. It's the farmer's market this weekend at Wyatt and Gabby's. It's the weekend before Christmas, and this one is bigger than their normal ones. I was going to see if you wanted to go. There will be pie." He winked.

With a chuckle, she nodded. "That sounds amazing."

"Okay."

He touched his lips to hers, coaxing them to part, and tightened his hold on her as the kiss deepened.

Being with him felt right. All the indecision she had about men would disappear when she thought about life with him.

She circled her arms around his neck, clinging to him as if he were a life preserver. Not because of anything he did, but because of his heart. She'd never met a man more gentle and kind. He'd rescued her when she'd lost her job, and now he was rescuing her by holding her when the earth under her feet felt like quicksand.

Her rule about dating had become a whispered nuisance in the back of her mind. It had been made with the intention of keeping Ellie from being hurt, but what she'd begun to realize was that it was her own heart she was worried about. How did she trust someone to hold it and not crush it?

She broke the kiss and set her forehead against his chest, trying to fill her air-deprived lungs. "These quality control checks are getting more serious."

"Yeah, they kinda are."

Something in his voice made her look at him. "What?"

Josiah chewed his bottom lip. "Nothing."

Molly narrowed her eyes. "That didn't sound like a nothing."

"How is a *nothing* supposed to sound?"

Shrugging, she said, "I don't know. But that was a Sarah Walker nothing, and we both know when she said nothing, it meant something."

"The fact that I can follow along with what you just said tells me I need to get out more." He laughed. "So? Farmer's market and pie?" A smile quirked on his lips, and she melted all over again. That smile. Anytime he looked at her like that, she expected to come away sunburned.

"You had me at pie." She snickered.

He kissed the tip of her nose. "That's a movie I haven't seen."

Her mouth dropped open. "We need to remedy that. It's a great movie."

"*Jerry Maguire* was about sports. I think we both know my talent lies with channel surfing on the couch."

She scoffed. "You should thank your lucky genetic stars for a metabolism that allows you to do that."

"Every cookie I eat, I do so in honor of my parents." Laughing, he stepped back. "Okay, getting ready." He gave her a quick peck on the lips and disappeared into his room.

Then it hit her. She liked him more than pie. Turning, she stepped inside her room and shut the door, wondering when that had happened. She would have rather stood in her bedroom doorway talking to Josiah than eating pie.

With a sigh, she ran her hand through her hair and shook her head. Even weirder was that he spoke her language. She'd acknowledged it before, but anyone can speak someone's language when they first meet. That was easy, but he was *still* speaking her language.

They'd had full-blown discussions in front of his family, and they'd all looked at the two of them like they were speaking in a foreign tongue. The movie references, music lyrics, video games…all of it.

Groaning, she squeezed her eyes shut, working to push away all the things running through her mind. She wasn't ready for a relationship. Not when she was fighting to keep Ellie. As if that wasn't stressful enough on its own, she was tempted to add a tiara, or in Molly's case, a relationship.

She pulled out the clothes she was going to wear, laying them on the bed, and then walked to the bathroom. Her heart was an *as-you-wish* away from winning the battle against her head.

Why was she even considering any of this? Yes, there was mutual kissing that had taken place, serious quality mutual kissing, but at this point, she couldn't be certain he wanted her or Ellie. Maybe he'd only kissed her because he felt sorry for her. Add to that, he didn't have many friends. What if he only kissed her because he was lonely and she was convenient? Worse, what if she'd only kissed him because she was stressed and needed a distraction? It didn't feel that way, but could she be sure of what she was feeling? The answer was no, even if the little voice in the back of her head said otherwise.

For the moment, she'd push it all away, go to the farmer's market, and enjoy herself. Hopefully, she could drown her doubts and sorrows with a pie. Something. Anything that would keep her mind from running in dizzying circles.

∽

Pausing at the entrance to the farmer's market, Molly inhaled and nearly went into a diabetic coma. Pie, cake, jellies, jams, cookies…she could see table after table of things she wanted to eat. Of course, pie was a given. The thread in her jeans was already locking arms in preparation for the smorgasbord of sweets she was going to consume.

"I should have worn my Thanksgiving pants," she said as she looked at Josiah. "Seriously, I could see moving here just to be close to this."

Nodding, Josiah said, "Uh, yeah. My couch-slouching days would be numbered if I lived here year-round." He waved, and Molly followed his line of sight and found Caroline and King walking toward them. King was holding Travis while Caroline held Ellie. Both were bundled up almost to *A Christmas Story* level. Good thing they weren't in the middle of potty training, or someone would be doing a lot of laundry.

As they approached, King smiled. "Look who's

here, Travis." Gabby's little boy grinned and leaned his head against King's shoulder. "What is this bashful business? You've never been shy a day in your life." King tickled the baby's tummy, and he giggled.

"Ellie is loving this," Caroline said. "She is just bright-eyed and looking around." Josiah's mom kissed Ellie's cheek. "Sweet girl."

Every time Molly thought she'd seen the depth of this family's kindness, she was shown it went further down than she could imagine. "Thank you for bringing Ellie."

Caroline handed her over to Molly. "Well, sure."

Molly laid her cheek against Ellie's, soaking her up. It crushed her to think Ellie could be taken from her. She hadn't known how much she could love someone until she held this tiny little person in her hands.

Josiah put his arm around her back, leaned in, and set his lips against Molly's ear. "I won't let her get taken."

She pressed her head against the side of Josiah's face. At that moment, she was surrounded by her two most favorite people in the world. It gave her a sense of belonging like she'd never had before.

"Thank you," she whispered…and quickly remembered his parents were right there. Watching them. Embarrassment climbed from her stomach and hit her ears faster than Mario avoiding barrels. Molly cast her gaze to the ground and wished the earth would swallow her whole.

"Okay, I think the three of us are going to go look around for a while," Josiah said as if sensing how awkward she felt.

"Sounds good. We'll see you…I guess when we see you. Have fun."

Molly waited until they'd walked a good distance and she was sure his parents were far enough away that she could relax. "Was it just me that felt…weird?" Was that even the right word?

He laughed. "Uh, I did a little? But I could see where your mind was going, and I cared more about that than feeling embarrassed. You're worried, and my parents understand that."

She nodded. "It's hard not to worry. That lawyer might be awesome, but this is Texas. The court system hates taking kids away from their birth parents to start with. Add in a single mom who works as a housekeeper and compare that to a stable older couple who are still rather young, and I just don't know how it'll turn out."

When he didn't say anything, she looked up at him. "What?"

He shrugged. "Nothing."

She leveled her eyes at him. "Really?"

"I have thoughts that I'm not…sure I should speak aloud. I like our friendship. I don't want to do anything that would either alienate you or jeopardize keeping you and Ellie in my life. It's not worth it to me."

Wrapping her fingers around his forearm, she pulled him to a stop. Before continuing the conversation, she laid Ellie in the stroller and buckled her in. "Okay, spill it."

Shaking his head, he said, "No way."

Molly pinched her lips together and put her hands on her hips. "Yes way."

"No." His voice went up an octave.

She looked around and then spotted exactly what she needed. "There's a pie-eating contest in an hour. I win; you spill. You win; you still spill."

His eyebrows knitted together. "How does that help me?"

"One way or another, you're going to tell me."

"Fine, but if I'm going to tell you, it'll be after the contest. Maybe the sugar high will work in my favor."

Her eyebrows lifted to her hairline. "That's where you're wrong!"

"I guess we'll see, huh?" He flashed a goofy smile, and she nearly sighed.

Sheesh, if she fell any harder for the guy, she'd need medical attention. What was happening to her? Just a few weeks ago, she was a single mom with zero thoughts of romance or interest. Now, she was staring down the shaft of Cupid's stupid arrow and peeking through her fingers as she waited for it to nail her right between the eyes.

She just needed to hold herself together until they got back to Dallas. Then she could have a little space, let things with Ellie settle down, and then see where she was. As she looked at him, though, the idea of a little space made her chest constrict. This was about as much space as she wanted. She was epically doomed.

CHAPTER 14

"I won fair and square," Josiah said, staring down Molly after the pie-eating contest was over. He hadn't won the contest, but he'd beat her by half a pie, and that was his only goal.

They'd gone back and forth while they were at the farmer's market, and the second they'd returned to the house, Molly had asked his mom to watch Ellie so she could "have a private word with him." It was like getting the look his dad would give if they were goofing off during church. Once he trained his gaze on you, you were done for.

What hadn't been part of his plan was to face down a fiery Molly Hines who had been clear what the rules were from the very beginning. Never mind that he'd not actually agreed to said rules.

Crossing her arms over her chest, she held his gaze. "Tell me now."

He raked his hand through his hair. It had been a wild millisecond thought. One that he didn't want to share and should never have mentioned. Granted, that was the second time he'd had the thought, but that only equaled two milliseconds. In his book, it still counted as not fully thought out. Definitely not to the point that he could share it.

She dropped her arms, crossed the room, and stopped in front of him, taking his face in her hands. "You are quite possibly the kindest, sweetest man I've ever known. Just tell me. It can't be that bad."

"I was just trying to figure out a way to get us in a better position to keep Ellie. It was an errant thought. Something neither of us is ready for." And he wasn't. More than anything, he knew Molly wasn't. Sharing a stupid, idle thought wasn't worth the risk of driving her away and losing her. "It was nothing."

Her eyes narrowed, and she balled his shirt in her hands. "Not nothing. Spill it, pie breath."

He pulled away and crossed the room. "I…I wondered if getting married would help. You could be a stay-at-home mom if you wanted. I definitely have the money to provide for both you and Ellie. We could buy a house in one of the suburbs of Dallas. I could even adopt Ellie with you."

Glancing at her, seeing the wide-eyed, horrified look on her face, made him cringe. He shouldn't have said anything. Why did he have to be the one West that couldn't play poker? "See? That's why I didn't want to tell you."

Molly palmed her forehead and took a deep breath. Josiah wondered if she would pass out at any moment. His idea wasn't just bad; it was something that shouldn't have been spoken aloud. It was the Voldemort of ideas.

"Wow," was all that came out of her mouth.

"I knew I shouldn't have said anything. Why can't I lie like a normal person? It would have made my life so much easier. Do you know how many times I was pummeled by my brothers and sister?" Sometimes, he wondered if there were lasting consequences. More than once, he'd chalked up his ability to remember useless trivia to the head trauma sustained as a child. That many poundings had to shake a wire loose.

Her hand dropped to her side, and she chewed her lip. "Actually, that idea kinda makes sense."

Now it was his turn to be floored. "What?"

"It's a good idea," she replied and then began pacing. "Well, other than the part where you adopt

Ellie. I mean, you'd be on the hook for child support." She stopped mid-stride and looked at him. "Otherwise, it's a pretty sound argument in favor of tying the knot."

Josiah shook his head and blinked. "Are you serious?"

"Are you?"

"Well, yeah, but how serious is your serious? Because my serious is extra serious." Then it caught up to him what he'd just proposed. Odd word choice for his brain to pick, but it fit.

She closed the distance between them and stopped in front of him. "I will do anything to keep Ellie." Her gaze drifted to the floor. "Anything," she whispered.

Of course, that would be the only reason she'd even consider being with him, but he was okay with that. For one, they hadn't even been on a proper date. Secondly, he had his career to think about. If he did manage to win Realtor of the Year, there was a chance he'd become really busy. Was it really a good idea to start a family just as his career was taking off?

Plus, they'd just really become friends, which was about as fast as either of them could go. The kissing put a weird spin on things, and he wasn't quite sure how to make that puzzle piece fit. He just knew it didn't translate to couple.

Marriage was a big deal, though. It was so much more than physical. It was sharing your heart and soul with someone. But this wasn't just about them anymore. A little girl was in the middle of this tug-of-war, and whatever advantages marriage gave them was worth it.

He wrapped his arms around her and pulled her against him. "We'll wait until the lawyer calls us back and go from there. If she thinks it's a good idea, then we'll do it."

As she lifted her gaze to his, they locked eyes. "That sounds like a good idea."

He'd also be talking to his dad, but Molly didn't need to know that. It wasn't so much that he was looking for approval as much as he was making sure he was considering all the ramifications of stepping up and being a husband and father. It was something he'd wanted, ached for at times even, but fatherhood wasn't just something that was happening to him. It was a choice he was making. Josiah was confident he could do it. Having his dad back him up was something extra to fortify his confidence.

"I don't know about you, but I could use some *Veronica Mars* and some downtime," he said.

A smile lifted the corners of Molly's lips. "Marshmallows unite." She laughed.

He winced. "Oh, don't mention food. I think I'm going to be sick as it is."

"I told you you'd get sick. It's like ordering tacos from that sushi place. It's just wrong." She shook her head. "And somehow the queso is always cold. Once is a fluke, but twice is food poisoning waiting to happen."

His eyebrows knitted together. "You know that place?"

"Well, yeah, they have tacos for fifty cents on Tuesdays. There is no little thing wrong with those… calling them tacos is sacrilegious." Narrowing her eyes, her mouth dropped open. "Oh my gosh, Josiah, don't tell me you ordered from that place?"

"Uh…" He rolled his lips and grimaced. "Maybe."

She gasped. "You did? Those things are lethal. Please tell me you didn't keep the menu."

When he'd considered a list of soulmate requirements, this had been pretty high on the list. If nothing else, marrying her would keep him from ordering from a host of Dallas area Chum Buckets.

A smile stretched on his lips. He could live with this. If they did get married, no, it wouldn't technically be real, but having someone to talk to, laugh with, and keep him from getting food poisoning was a plus. People had married for less noble reasons.

Josiah kissed her and hugged her tight. Yeah, this could work...if they had to marry. He'd just need to remember she didn't really want him as much as she wanted to keep Ellie. While it stung a little, he understood that. And there was always the possibility of things changing in the future. He'd just hold on to that hope.

∼

THE SUN WAS SITTING dead center on the horizon as Josiah walked from the house to the barn. In an effort to give himself some space to think, he'd volunteered to clean the feed room in the barn. It garnered him some strange looks, but it had been worth it to get a moment of quiet to think.

Not that he'd been doing much other than that since he'd told Molly about his idea to get married. With it being Christmas Eve, it would be several more days before the lawyer called, and it seemed that all his mind wanted to do was run in circles.

He'd planned to talk to his dad, but every time he tried, it wouldn't come out. How, exactly, could he start a conversation like that? His parents thought of marriage as sacred, and they'd instilled that into Josiah and all of his siblings. Marriage wasn't something you did on a whim or to fix a problem. It was a commitment to another person, and not once did you enter it with the idea that divorce was an option. Whether they would end it was probably something they needed to discuss at some point.

"Josiah!" With the sound of his name, he turned and found Bear quickly catching up to him. "Hey, I thought I'd help."

Josiah eyed him. "Yeah, right. You just don't trust me to do it the way you would."

His brother stuffed his hands in his coat pockets and shrugged. "I live here. You don't. May as well be the way I want things done."

Okay, so he had a point, but the idea of cleaning the feed room was to get away and think. Not to be hounded about every detail. "How about you give me a quick tutorial, and I'll do it?"

"How about we work on it together, and you tell me what's eating you?" His brother smiled.

"Why can't a guy just get some peace?"

Bear stopped him as they reached the barn. "That little girl is sweet as can be, and I know the idea that someone could come along and take her is worrisome to you."

"I don't want her taken from Molly *or* me."

"I know." Bear pulled the barn door open, stepped

inside, and waited for Josiah to follow him in before shutting it behind them. "I can't fathom how Molly's feeling. Birth momma or not, she's been taking care of her, getting up at night with her, loving her."

"Exactly," Josiah replied. "Why would her mom want to do that? What purpose does it serve to take Ellie and lose Molly? Because that's what will happen. It will irrevocably harm their relationship."

Bear faced him and leaned his shoulder against the wall. "It could also mean you getting your heart broken."

Josiah balked. "Me? No, I'm fine. It's Molly I'm worried about."

Rubbing his knuckles along his jaw, Bear's gaze drifted to the floor. A few minutes passed, and finally he lifted his gaze to Josiah's. "I've seen how you look at her. You're as lovesick as they come. Probably have been and didn't even know it. Ain't no other explanation for you inviting her home for Christmas. It might have been buried in that brain of yours, but you've liked her since you met her. You may have helped her out by giving her a job, but there was something there from the get-go."

"You've been spending too much time around Dad." Before Josiah invited Molly home, they'd only really talked after she was finished cleaning his not-so-messy apartment.

"Maybe, but that doesn't make me wrong. Listen, I get it. She's a pretty little thing. She speaks the same weird movie-song-lyric language as you. She's sweet as all get-out, and funny. If she wasn't with you, I'd be seriously looking in her direction." Bear grinned. "So, why did you volunteer to clean my feed room the day before Christmas? There's a very hot place covered in a thick sheet of ice right now, and I want to know why."

Josiah huffed and crossed his arms over his chest. "Just because I volunteer to do manual labor doesn't mean something is up."

Bear waved him off and straightened. "You can shovel that somewhere else. Now, I know something's up."

"I told her we should get married in order to give us a better chance at keeping Ellie." It flew out of his mouth before he could stop himself.

"Married? Josiah…man, that ain't no small thing. You ready to be a daddy? Because that little baby is an innocent bystander in all this. The second you decide to step into that role, you can't take it back."

"I wouldn't want to take it back." Josiah raked his hand through his hair. "Bear, I love that little girl. I know it's not all fun and that taking care of her is a commitment that lasts a lifetime, but I *want* her."

"But marrying her momma? Is that something you really want to do?"

"I don't know." Which is why he wanted peace and quiet to think. So he could figure out a few things. It felt like he had to choose between his career and having a family. A decision he wasn't sure he was ready to make.

Bear eyed him. "Be honest, Josiah. There's no shame in having feelings for her."

Josiah's gaze dropped to the floor. "She doesn't feel that way about me. The only reason she'd be marrying me is to keep Ellie."

"That's not what I asked." Bear popped him on the shoulder. "Answer the question and answer it honestly."

"Yes…" he said, swallowing hard as the answer came out in a burst. "I want to marry her."

"Now we're getting somewhere. Do you love her?"

Nodding, Josiah lifted his gaze to Bear's. If he was honest, he loved her more than anything. Yes, he wanted Realtor of the Year, but he also wanted Molly. He just didn't know how to balance it. He didn't even know if it was an option.

"Yeah. But she doesn't feel that way about me, and I

need to just not think about that. I need to keep myself prepared for the possibility that she'll never feel that way about me," Josiah replied.

Bear took a deep breath. "Are you okay with that? And don't give me bull, because you can't tell a lie to save your life."

Talk about a tough question. That was at the heart of all his thoughts. Could he be okay with that? What if Molly never felt about him the way he felt about her? Sure, they could get a divorce later on, but he wasn't sure he could stomach getting married and knowing they'd be ending it sometime down the line.

"I don't know, Bear. That's what's been bugging me since I suggested it. But I can't go back on it. I mean, I could, but I don't want to hurt Molly." And now he felt like a lowlife for even having all those thoughts. He'd said he'd do whatever it took to keep Ellie. Now all he could do was question it.

"Yeah, it would be a tough thing to do." Bear nodded. "That is, if I thought those feelings were one-sided. Thing is, I've seen how she looks at you, too."

Josiah grumbled, "Then why go through all this interrogation?"

Smiling, Bear said, "Because you needed to hear your thoughts out loud. I've got no advice on any of it, but I know you. You'll do the right thing."

The right thing. Keeping his word to Molly or protecting himself? How could he choose himself when a baby was in the middle of it? He couldn't. At least, he didn't think so. Hopefully, by the time the lawyer called, Josiah would have a solid answer. Maybe hiring the lawyer would make Molly's mom rethink taking Ellie, and all the worrying would be for nothing.

CHAPTER 15

Sauntering into the kitchen, Molly went straight to the sink and washed her rag out. She'd gotten up before dawn to clean the house before everyone woke up for Christmas. Josiah wasn't the only one who had a love language. Yes, there were gifts under the tree for everyone, but they were purchased with Josiah's money. Molly needed her own gift to give.

Mostly, her sleeplessness was due to his proposal. She hadn't expected that at all. It had made sense to her, but it was a big deal. He'd even offered to adopt Ellie, not even flinching when she'd said he'd be forced to provide child support. He'd just offered his life to her so she could keep her baby. What kind of man did that? None that she'd met before him.

Still, it was marriage and adoption, and it was a lot to consider. Would the marriage end one day? When? How did that get decided?

"Wh-wh-what are y-y-you doing?" asked Bandit.

Molly startled and blew out a big breath as she leaned her stomach against the counter. "You scared the daylights out of me!"

Bandit's cheeks turned pink, and he lowered his gaze. "I'm s-s-sorry."

Talk about a sweet, cute guy. It had been a shock to find out he wasn't a member of the West family. He looked so much like them—tall, dark hair, strong jawline. He fit perfectly.

"It's okay. I thought I'd clean the house to get it ready for Christmas," she replied.

He lifted his gaze and looked around. "Looks gr-gr-great."

She shrugged. "Thanks. I was just rinsing out this rag, and I'll be out of your hair."

He shook his head. "N-n-nah, you're fine."

Just as he finished the statement, a yawning Reagan entered the kitchen. "I'm sorry. I'll get the coffee going."

"Now, that is worth getting up early for," Molly said as she wrung out the rag she'd been using. "Where should I put this?"

"L-l-lay it on th-th-the sink. I'm sure I'll need it later," Bandit replied. "I'm going to ch-ch-check the firewood and m-m-make sure there's enough for the d-d-day."

As he left the kitchen, Molly parked herself on a stool at the island. "You make the best coffee I've ever tasted."

Reagan laughed. "Thanks. I've always just thought of it as coffee. It wasn't until I got here that I was told it was great."

"Well, it is. Like, secret-ingredient, crave-for-it-nightly great," Molly said with the best Scottish accent she could muster.

"That's funny. Sounds similar to something Josiah once said." Reagan finished getting the coffee ready to brew and leaned her hip against the counter. "You two make a good couple."

Molly's eyes widened. "We're not…" They weren't a couple. They took care of Ellie together and kissed…a lot. But that didn't mean they were a couple. Just friends with lucrative kissing benefits.

Reagan held her hand up. "You're talking to the woman who pretended to be a man's fiancée. Of all the people in this house, I am uniquely qualified to call your bluff on that."

"He's just helping me with Ellie. He's the baby whisperer."

"You look at Josiah the same way I looked at Hunter." She smiled. "You may not want to admit it, but you know I'm right."

Molly hung her head. "I can't date, Reagan. After all I went through as a kid, the way my mom dated. I don't want that for Ellie."

"That's a fair point, but do you really think Josiah is the kind of man to walk out? Is it really Ellie you're worried about, or is it yourself?"

Molly lifted her head and began to protest. "I'm—"

"I'm not judging, because I've been there. Admitting that I loved Hunter meant that getting hurt was a real possibility. No one in their right mind wants to be hurt, and I'm imagining that's especially true when you have a baby to consider."

What could Molly say? The truth was, she *was* afraid of being hurt. She was afraid of leaning on someone, allowing Ellie to lean on someone, and risking their hearts. What if Josiah decided in five or six years that he'd had all the fathering he could handle? What then? Even adopting her, he could wash his hands of her. Just like Molly's biological father. He'd found a new wife and then a new life with three kids.

Reagan covered Molly's hand with hers. "Listen, it's scary trusting people. It's even scarier trusting yourself. I know from experience."

"Yeah?" Molly's stomach was twisted in knots.

The last thing she wanted was to hurt Josiah. He'd been more than wonderful to her, but what if it wasn't Ellie he quit? What if it was Molly? Could she withstand being abandoned again?

"No one can make these choices for you. No one can change you either. It was a hard lesson I had to learn. I needed to change because I didn't want to live in the past. Yes, there's a chance Hunter could hurt me in the future, but there's also a chance he won't. I had to decide that I wanted Hunter more than I wanted safety."

"Do you still feel like that?"

Shaking her head, Reagan said, "Actually, what I've found is that I'm safer with Hunter than I am alone. I'm not saying either one of us is perfect, but when it comes to having each other's backs, I can count on him."

Molly did like the sound of that. She'd been on her own so long that it was all she knew. The idea that she could depend on someone was both exciting and scary. "If I tell you something, will you keep it a secret?"

"Well, it would depend on the secret."

"Josiah suggested we get married as a way to keep Ellie." Molly paused a moment to gauge Reagan's reaction. "I have to admit it's tempting, but I don't want to use him like that."

"Wow. That's…wow." Reagan pulled open a cupboard and took out two cups, pouring one for Molly and then herself. "Sweet, though. Josiah loves Ellie…and I think he feels the same about her mom."

Waving her off, Molly stood, went to the fridge, and pulled out the cream. "No, we're friends. Before this…" Before this what? She always found a reason to stick around until he got home on the days she cleaned his apartment.

She'd known from the very beginning that he'd hired her because he found her crying. It had been the elephant in the room from the start, and he'd confirmed it on the drive to Caprock Canyon. Who wouldn't have a crush on a man who did that?

Plus, sheesh, he was cute. She'd thought that the second she saw him that day in the coffee shop, and if she was being honest with herself, he'd been the reason she'd gotten that order wrong. She'd still been ogling Josiah when the next customer ordered.

Reagan grinned. "Yeah, before this, there was already something brewing. Josiah is a good guy. He's sweet and funny. Part of the time, I get his movie and song references, but you two? It's like you speak Elven or something."

"Josiah is a fantastic guy." That wasn't even debatable. He was the most incredible man she'd ever met, and she did care about him. But this was about more than just them. It was about Ellie too. No, Molly didn't want to get hurt, but more than anything, she didn't want her little girl to get hurt like Molly was the day her dad packed. He was going to keep in touch. Nothing was going to change, and he still loved her.

But it was a lie. It may not have been an intentional lie when her dad made the promises, but he'd broken them just the same. He didn't keep in touch. Everything changed, and she'd been left picking up the pieces like breadcrumbs, trying to find her way back to normal—something that didn't exist anymore.

"Good morning, ladies." King smiled as he walked into the kitchen, grabbed a cup from the cabinet, and held it out as Reagan filled it. "Thank you." He looked at Molly. "She's one of my favorite kids." He looked back at Reagan and winked.

Rolling her eyes, Reagan took a sip of her coffee. "He always says that. It's the coffee." She laughed.

"Nah, it's the coffee maker." He laughed and took a

seat next to Molly, patting her on the back. "How are you doing this morning?"

"I'm okay. All things considered."

"That's about all you can be. Josiah said you've got a Tasmanian devil for a lawyer, so that's got to help a little."

A little? "No, it helps a ton. I just wish I could understand my mom." Not just that, but was Molly a bad mom? She'd been asking herself that since the conversation with her mom.

She and Ellie didn't have a big apartment. She couldn't be a stay-at-home mom because she had to work. There was no big back yard or great school in the suburbs. Were those the things that made a mom great?

Molly's mom had worked. They were in just a so-so school district. They lived in a house, but they moved not long after her dad left. Molly didn't think of her mom as a bad mom at the time.

"I've got no answers for that. I won't judge another person's parentage. At some point, we've all failed." King took a drink of his coffee and groaned. "Oh, Reagan, I think this is your best pot yet."

"You say that every time." Reagan laughed.

"It's true every time."

Hunter strolled in, dressed in jeans and a t-shirt,

and stopped by Reagan. "Hey." He smiled, put his arm around, and kissed her. "Good morning."

Reagan leaned into him. "Hi."

Molly's envy factor tripled. She wanted that so badly, but was she ready to be the person someone could lean on? Granted, she'd taken on the responsibility of taking care of Ellie, but that was a different kind of commitment than a relationship and love and marriage.

"I think I'm going to go check on Ellie," Molly said and stood, quickly setting her cup in the sink and leaving.

As she reached the top landing, she paused as she heard singing coming from the end of the hall. Following it, she tiptoed down the hall and stopped at her room. She had the monitor in her pocket, but she'd not heard Ellie at all.

Leaning against the doorway, her heart melted as she listened to Josiah singing to Ellie. She knew the melody, "Goodnight, my Angel," but he was changing the words.

"Good morning, darling, now we're both awake, and I can't wait for the smiles you'll make. My promise is to never leave and cherish moments just like these. Your tiny laughter is the greatest prize a father could ever want to hear. These lyrics are a horrible mess, but

I don't care because you can't understand." He sang the last sentence as off-key as possible, and Molly held in a giggle.

Josiah stopped humming and held Ellie up in front of him. "You are the tiniest, cutest person in the whole world, but that's just between us. Okay? My brother Wyatt would disagree, and I'd hate to throw down with him." He brought her close and kissed her. "And since I'm a lover and not a fighter, a fight would just end with me having a lot of bruises."

Before Molly could announce herself, Josiah sighed and brought Ellie close to his face. "I sure do love you. I hope you know that despite my singing. We probably should have your hearing checked the next time you visit the pediatrician. For that, I'm truly sorry." He grinned.

He loved Ellie, not Molly. Sure, they were kissing a whole lot, but how long had it been since she'd kissed someone? The last couple of months had been hard on her as she learned to balance work and being a mom. Everything she was feeling could be explained away as loneliness and stress.

Reagan meant well, but she was wrong. What she saw between Molly and Josiah wasn't feelings as in dating or otherwise. It was two extremely lonely people finding common ground and using the other person to satisfy the need for companionship. There was nothing more to it.

Molly didn't need to worry about her heart being broken or leaning on someone. As soon as the holidays were over, she'd keep in touch for Ellie's sake, but whatever was going on between her and Josiah would be over as soon as they were back in Dallas and reality hit. With the pressure from her mom, did she really need to add relationship questions on top of it?

Taking a deep breath, she closed her eyes and stilled her mind. It was Christmas Day. A day to relax and enjoy the present with presents. That's what she was going to do. Cast worry aside and focus on the now.

CHAPTER 16

With Molly sitting next to Josiah, holding Ellie, it was easy for him to picture his life. Well, with maybe a couple more kids and even maybe a cat. Hunter and Reagan's Great Dane was cool, but picking up after it? Uh, no, thanks.

Molly shifted Ellie from one arm to the other, and the conversation he'd overheard returned in stereo. He'd listened to Molly and Reagan talking for a minute and gone back upstairs to tend to Ellie so Molly could have her conversation without being interrupted.

She'd said he was fantastic…and just a friend. He'd known that, but hearing it was disappointing. He wasn't even sure that was the right word for it. Expected? Maybe that was a better word.

After his talk with Bear, he'd allowed himself to get his hopes up about maybe having something with Molly. So much so that, if he was truthful, it was more than disappointing. More like heart-piercing.

He'd even reconsidered the whole marriage suggestion…until he held Ellie. As much as he loved her, he knew Molly loved her even more. He couldn't go back on his promise to do everything he could to keep Ellie from being taken. It wasn't like the whole marriage thing was set in stone anyway. If the lawyer didn't see a reason for it, they wouldn't.

"Josiah?"

The sound of Molly's voice broke through his thoughts, and he looked at her. "Uh, sorry."

His dad held up a gift and laughed. "You must have been thinking awful hard if you didn't hear me call your name." He passed the gift to Wyatt, and it slowly reached Josiah.

He shook his head. "No, just relaxing."

His dad eyed him for a second. "If you say so."

After tearing the paper off the gift, Josiah pulled on the corners of the box until it popped. A smile formed on his lips as he plucked the gift out, and he laughed. "A Mr. Matchmaker cruise to Alaska?" He grabbed the wrapping and checked the name on the gift tag. "Carrie Anne, what is this?"

"It's exactly what it says." She chuckled. "Open it."

He kept his gaze trained on Carrie Anne as he pulled the brochure open. "Really? You're not funny." Two season tickets to the Rangers' baseball games were hidden inside. "You're not funny at all."

Everyone busted out laughing except Bear and Josiah. Bear grumbled and stood. "He's right. That's not even a little funny."

Carrie Anne quickly jumped up. "Bear, it was funny. All I did was make the profile, and it was only up on the site a tiny little bit. You went on one single date. Are you ever going to forgive me?"

Their dad stood and stepped in between them. "Listen here," he said, turning to Bear. "This has gone on long enough—"

"But—"

"Hush, I'm speaking. It's gone on long enough. Now, Bear, I get being upset. You had every right to be mad, but that was a while ago now, and Carrie Anne has apologized plenty. Accept the apology."

Bear pinched his lips closed and shook his head. "Fine. Apology accepted."

"And, Carrie Anne," their dad said and turned to her. "If you want to do this matchmaking stuff, that's fine, but open a business and do it. That way you're not meddling where you shouldn't be.

Attempting to put Bear on that website was wrong. Apologize—"

"I—"

"Yes, *but*…That's what you've used. You've apologized and hooked a reason to it. An apology is given without any strings or vindication or reasoning. It's just an apology. Now, give Bear a real apology."

Her shoulders sagged. "Bear, I'm sorry. I didn't mean to make you so mad or hurt you. I love you, and I want you happy…whatever that might mean to you."

Wow. It was about time, but Josiah was surprised it was taking place during Christmas. Usually, this sort of stuff was left to work itself out, but in Bear's case, it was going to take work to get him simmered down.

Bear rubbed his face with his hands. "I'm not unhappy. Just don't do that again." He pulled Carrie Anne into a hug. "I know it was out of love, but I can find my own dates." He held her out from him. "Now, tell everyone your news."

News? Josiah looked from Bear to Carrie Anne.

She grinned. "It's official. I'm pregnant."

Everyone clapped and cheered, scaring Ellie and Travis. Both babies broke out in wails, and the family quickly calmed down.

Handing Ellie to Josiah, Molly said, "As far as

Christmases go, this one is kind of exciting. Ours usually ended with my brother and me watching TV."

"It's not typically like this. Although, last year Gabby announced she was pregnant." He paused a minute. Now that he thought about it, Christmas was probably never going to be the same again. "I guess they're going to be different from now on with my brothers and my sister being married, having kids." He looked down at Ellie. "That's okay, though. I can picture Ellie when she's a little older, tearing open gifts, her eyes sparkling."

Molly leaned her shoulder against his. "Can't say I haven't pictured the same thing. I don't want to spoil her with things, but I think it's fun to watch kids open gifts."

"Yeah."

"Hey," she said, dipping her head to catch his gaze. "Are you okay?"

Nodding, he said, "I'm fine." He smiled. It wasn't totally untrue. Mostly, he was, well, he didn't know exactly what he was. Maybe a little heartsick to see his siblings so blissfully happy, excited about their futures, while he was wondering if he was ever going to have that.

Sure, he'd agreed to marry Molly, but it was a marriage on paper. Nothing more. It wasn't friendship, love, and commitment. Not the things he'd been taught that were important in a relationship.

Shaking his head, he cleared his thoughts. It was Christmas. Not the time to be thinking deep. He'd worry about all that stuff later. For now, he'd be happy with what he had.

CHAPTER 17

The day after Christmas, Molly and Josiah were in the study speaking with Ms. Salinas. It had been a shock when she called during breakfast. They'd left Ellie with Carrie Anne and quickly went to the study so they could actually hear her.

"Okay. After spending some time going over the case, I think we have a good shot. Not great, but good. Texas judges don't like terminating parental rights. So, if Brenda wants to change her mind, they're likely to listen."

Molly's heart dropped to the floor. "So…Brenda can take her back?" She'd tried every number she'd had for Brenda, and either they were disconnected or it was the wrong number. She'd even tried to call Derek, but he wouldn't answer his phone.

"She can. However, after speaking to the doctor who delivered Ellie, I think we can convince the court that she didn't want Ellie. The OB who delivered Ellie backed up your statement that Brenda didn't even want to touch her."

Molly chewed her thumb as she stood in front of the desk. "She didn't. Even my mom wouldn't take her. They handed Ellie to my brother, and he almost threw her into my arms."

Papers shuffling filtered through the phone. "Do you have any idea what might have happened in the last few weeks to make Brenda or your brother change their minds?"

"Molly said she thinks her mom might have offered them money, but we wouldn't know how to prove that," Josiah said as he put his arm around Molly.

"Well, I'm not sure we could use that anyway. It wouldn't be difficult to explain giving money to her son. Now, Brenda, on the other hand…that would be a little more difficult. We'd have to show cause, though, if we wanted to subpoena the Hines's financial records."

"Maybe we could try calling your brother again?" Josiah shrugged as he looked at Molly.

"Maybe." Molly dropped her thumb from her mouth. "I'm not sure he'd be truthful with me even if my mom did give him money. I mean, I'd cut ties with him because he stole my credit card."

Another call popped up on the screen of Josiah's phone as it lay on the desk in front of them. He pulled free of Molly and picked it up. Raking his hand through his hair, he grumbled something Molly couldn't make out.

Since the pie tasting, Josiah hadn't had any more work emergencies. It didn't keep the little doubts from bubbling up from time to time, but she continued to remind herself that they weren't dating. She'd been the one to put that line in the sand, not him. Then again, she'd slowly been using her toe to bury it. It was a never-ending mental battle that left her ready for bed at the end of the day.

"It's work. I need to answer this really quick," Josiah said as he held Molly's gaze. "Ms. Salinas, I need to put you on hold just a second. I'll be right back."

"Sure," Ms. Salinas said.

Molly nodded, but the little insecurities she'd felt from before roared back to life. This wasn't just a pie tasting. It was about Ellie, and he was putting it on hold for what? What could be more important than someone he loved?

He switched calls and stuck his hand in his pocket. "Hey…I know. I'm on another call at the moment. Let me finish with it, and you can have my full attention after."

After a few more seconds of conversation, Josiah switched back to Ms. Salinas. "We're back. Sorry about that."

"No problem. Work is life, right?"

"Pretty much." He chuckled.

Only, Molly didn't think it was funny. Work is life? Where did that put Ellie on his list? Second? Third? Tenth? How could Molly trust him to be there for Ellie when his job came first?

"Uh, we were wondering if it would help our chances with Ellie to…maybe…get married." As he said it, the volume of his voice lowered.

Molly studied him, wondering if he'd decided that getting married wasn't something he really wanted to do. Not that she thought it would be a real marriage, but a tiny part of her had wondered if it could be…one day.

The attorney took a deep breath. "I don't think so. I mean, if you want to get married, go ahead, but I'm not sure a judge would consider that. More than anything, talking to Brenda and Derek would be the best course of action."

The fact that he looked almost relieved hurt Molly in ways she didn't think possible. But this was what happened when you trusted people. They let you down. It didn't matter how true their intention might have been, because that didn't change the results.

Molly turned away from him and blinked back the stupid tears that threatened. Why did she have to be so sappy and weak? It wasn't like she didn't know this would happen.

"I've spoken to your mother's attorney, and I've filed an extension with the court to postpone the current court date so we have time to prepare. The judge is going to consider what's in the best interest of the child. He's going to listen to everyone involved, ask a lot of questions, and then make his decision." She paused. "The fact that Ellie has been living with you this long will help. Plus, having me in your corner. If Brenda didn't want her and she specifically asked you to take her, the question on everyone's mind will be: why did she change her mind?"

Molly took a deep breath. This wasn't the time to be falling apart over a relationship that didn't even exist. Ellie needed her to hold it together. She turned and faced Josiah. "Be straight with me. Do you really think I have a chance at keeping Ellie? Selfishly, I want to fight for her, but I don't want to do that if there's no chance."

The attorney waited a few breaths before replying,

"I think you have a good chance. If I were you, I'd be hoping for the best and preparing for the worst. I'd also be trying to talk to Ellie's biological mother and find out what happened."

"Okay," Josiah said. "We'll see what we can do to find her and Derek."

"Sounds good. I'll contact you when I know the response to the extension."

They concluded the call, and Josiah closed the distance between himself and Molly. "She's lived with you this long. I'm not sure how it would be in her best interest to take her from the only mom she knows."

"I hope so."

"We could still get married. It can't hurt our chances."

No, but it could break her heart. "Ms. Salinas said that wouldn't make a difference. Plus, you said yourself that you work a lot. 'Work is life,' right? I mean, I'm already taking you away from client calls."

For heartbeat after heartbeat, Josiah held her gaze. It seemed he was warring with himself. "Yeah, now that you mention it, I probably need to call them back." He hugged her to him. "I'll try to make it quick."

"No rush. I think I'll take Ellie for a walk."

"Okay," he said and smiled. "I'll see you in a bit."

Molly watched as he left the study and then sank

into a nearby chair. How many times had she watched men walk out of her life? When she was a kid, she had no choice. As an adult, even when she'd had a choice, it had been the wrong one. At least, so far it had.

This time was different. She was done being the sad sap who watched people walk out of her life. This time, she was going to be the one doing the walking. It wasn't a decision she'd make lightly, though. She'd take Ellie on a walk, let her emotions settle, and then she'd slowly pull away from Josiah. Unlike the people in her life, she wouldn't blindside him. By the time they got back to Dallas, it would be as if the trip never happened. He could go his way, and she could go hers. It was best for everyone.

CHAPTER 18

Josiah hated ditching Molly when he did, but he couldn't ignore Malakai's call. During their last conversation, it came out that the singer knew a private detective in Dallas. He was supposed to be calling Josiah back with details about whether the woman was taking new clients.

He pulled on his coat, stepped out into the cold, and hit the call button on his phone as he reached his pickup and slid inside.

"Hey, Josiah."

"Hey, I'm sorry. We were talking to the lawyer." He paused as he got in the truck. "She thinks we need to talk to Derek and Brenda too."

Apparently, the phone was on speaker, because the next voice belonged to a woman. "Josiah West, this is

Emilia Sanger. Malakai gave me a few details, and I'd like to help."

"Hi, Ms. Sanger—"

"Emilia, please." She chuckled.

"Emilia, thank you."

He started from the beginning, detailing everything he knew: where Derek and Brenda were last seen and Molly's suspicion that her mom was paying them to change their minds.

He'd debated about telling Molly what he was doing, but for one, he wasn't sure Emilia would even take the case. Plus, he didn't want to get Molly's hopes up that they'd find Brenda only to come up empty. Molly was already dealing with enough; he didn't want to add another disappointment to the list.

"Oh, man, her mom?" Malakai whistled. "That's harsh."

"Yeah, that's what I thought," Josiah replied.

"So, Derek and Brenda are here in Dallas. Do her parents live in Dallas?" Emilia asked.

Josiah nodded. "Yeah, in the Flower Mound area."

"Nice neighborhood and good schools," she added.

"Can't deny that, but trying to take her granddaughter at the expense of her daughter isn't so great." Josiah still couldn't wrap his mind around that.

"No, it's not. Okay, do you have a physical description of them?"

Josiah grumbled. Why hadn't he thought of that? He should have been prepared for it in case she did take the case. "No, but I can get them and then text it to you."

"Awesome. I'll get you my fee schedule, and once you agree to that, you can send me the photos. I'll get to work on it." It sounded to Josiah like she was farther from the phone this time.

"Okay."

"I'll talk to you later, Mal," she said, and then a door opened and shut.

"Hey, Josiah," Malakai said quickly like he thought Josiah was hanging up. "While you're on the phone, I wanted to go over that list of properties you sent me the other day."

"You bet. Did you like any of them?"

"I liked that third one. Tyler wants to know if there's ever been a restaurant in that location."

Josiah pulled up the property on his phone and scrolled through his notes. "Not that I can see. I'm looking through all the records. It's been a clothing store, a fabric store, and an art studio. No restaurants."

"Art studio. That's cool. Do you think we could go look at it in a couple of days?"

Josiah pulled up his calendar. "I'd love to, but…"

"Oh, man, yeah. Your girl is stressing. Man, I'm sorry. I wasn't even thinking."

Chuckling, Josiah shook his head. "She's not really my girl, but I do need to stay. I can get another realtor to show you the space, though. It's not a big deal."

"That's fine with me. You've been great. Emilia is awesome. If she can't find someone, they can't be found by anyone."

"Good to know. Anyway, I need to get back. If you need anything…"

"Text me your dude's number. Go be with your family."

They said their goodbyes, and Josiah ended the call. He stepped out of the truck and found his dad sitting on the porch with a mug in his hand.

"Hey, bud. Why don't you come sit a spell with me?"

Josiah took the stairs two at a time and took a seat in the rocking chair next to his dad. "What's up, Dad?"

"Oh, not much. Just enjoying the quiet."

Josiah rolled his eyes. That was the most ominous *not much* he'd ever heard. "I guess it *is* noisy in there."

"Not too bad, but not as quiet as it used to be." He smiled.

As the silence lingered, Josiah relaxed and let his

gaze roam over the scene in front of him: horses in the pasture, his breath coming out in little white puffs, and nothing and no one for miles. It was peaceful and maddening all at once for someone used to living in the city.

"Son, I'm not sure when you decided your mom and I weren't proud of you, but, bud, I am."

"I know."

His dad looked at him and laughed. "Son, never step foot in Vegas."

Josiah waved him off. "Whatever."

"Listen, bud," he said and sat forward, tapping Josiah on the leg. "Your momma and I are proud of you."

"Really? Because I'm not a rodeo star or a great house flipper or a ranch owner or Teacher of the Year. None of that. I'm just a real estate agent, and that's it."

"That's it, huh?"

Shrugging, Josiah nodded. "Yeah, that's it."

His dad shook his head. "You hired Molly because someone was cruel to her. You invited her home when you found out she didn't have anywhere to go. You paid those layaways off and gave the hospital in Dallas a huge donation."

Josiah's eyes widened. "How do you know that?"

"Because I'm your daddy, and I know you." He

patted Josiah's back. "You've got your success where it matters, bud. I'm not discounting that Realtor of the Year award, but I can't see it making you happy."

Was there anything his parents didn't know? "I haven't even said anything about that award."

"No, but you wouldn't be working so hard if there wasn't something at the end waiting for you. My question is, is that the something you want?"

More and more, that had been the thing plaguing his mind. Until a few weeks ago, he would have wholeheartedly said yes. It had been important to him, but now it felt so empty. What would he have after that? A nice award but no one at home.

"I can tell by the look on your face that it's not," his dad said.

"I thought it was what I wanted. I just…I needed to feel successful. Compared to—"

His dad lifted his hand and cut him off. "Stop comparing yourself. Wyatt thought he was happy with the rodeo. He wasn't. Hunter thought he was happy with his flipping business. He wasn't. It was great that Carrie Anne won her award, but she loves her job and being around kids. It wasn't things that made them happy; it was love."

Josiah hadn't thought about it like that, but it was true. Both his brothers had success, and it hadn't fulfilled them. Finding love had. All this time, Josiah had been looking at things totally wrong. Did he really care about Realtor of the Year? No. It was a lot of work and long, lonely nights.

He loved pizza, movies, and hanging out. Not that he wanted to quit his job, but it wasn't the piece he was missing. It wasn't even close. "I'm in love with Molly. I love Ellie. All I want is them."

His dad pointed his finger at him. "That's my boy."

"Thanks, Dad."

"You're welcome." He sat back and took a long drag of his drink. "Remember, though, you hurt my grandbaby, and I'll take a stick to you."

Laughing, Josiah stood and walked to the door. "I think I've stayed too far from home. Maybe I need to see what the real estate market looks like in Caprock Canyon. If Molly wants to stay in Dallas, that's where I'll be, but if she's willing…"

"Don't hurt to ask."

"Thanks again, Dad," he said as he opened the door and stepped inside.

As he shrugged out of his coat, he realized he was more at peace than he'd been in a long while. The award was great, and he was sure he'd still get the nomination. If he won, great. If not, that was fine too. He wasn't giving his life to it any longer.

He'd watch his little girl walk across the stage to receive her diploma. Walk her down the aisle. Be a grandpa to her child. That's what he'd count as success. Loving her, teaching her to love, and being there for her.

The same would go for her mom. Molly needed someone to walk toward her for once. He could be that guy if she gave him the chance. If his phone rang again for work, they could leave a message.

CHAPTER 19

With her hands in her lap, Molly kept her gaze trained on the road in front of her. "Are you really not going to tell me why we drove all the way to Lubbock?"

She and Josiah had left early that morning with the hopes of getting back so they could celebrate New Year's Eve with his family. It seemed odd that he'd pick this day for a road trip. They'd left Ellie with his mom and dad, and the cab of the truck was weirdly quiet.

Shaking his head, Josiah shot her a glance and smiled. "Nope. It's a surprise."

Since their conversation with the lawyer, Molly had slowly put a little distance between her and Josiah. There were no more kisses or snuggling. They still laughed and joked, but that's where she drew the line.

After taking Ellie for a walk, she'd come back to the house with a clear head and a solid plan. She appreciated what Josiah was doing for her, and she'd always be grateful. But the fanciful notions of a relationship were over. He loved his job more than he loved anything or anyone. That wasn't the life Molly wanted for Ellie. Someone straddling the fence between work and family and choosing work more often than not wasn't enough.

They passed the Lubbock Country Club and continued on until they turned into a city park named Mackenzie with signs pointing them in the direction of Prairie Dog Town. Surely, that wasn't what they were here for.

Craning her neck, Molly tried to figure out why he would have brought her here. Then her jaw dropped as Brenda came into view. "Ellie's mom?"

"I hired a private detective to find her. I wanted to tell you, but at the time, I didn't know if the detective would take the case or if they could even find Brenda. I didn't want to get your hopes up just to see them crushed." He glanced at her. "I'm sorry."

Molly didn't know if she was mad or glad or what. It bothered her that he didn't include her, but he'd found Ellie's birth mom. That's what mattered. "I'm just glad we can talk to her."

Josiah grinned as he parked the truck, and they got out. As he reached Brenda, he shook her hand. "Hi, Brenda. I'm Josiah West."

Brenda smiled at Molly and then hugged her. "Hey, Molly."

"Hey," Molly replied and leaned back. "What are you doing in Lubbock?"

"I'm from Lubbock. I missed my family, and my dad offered to help me get back into school. I'm taking a few classes at South Plains College so I can transfer to Tech after."

Molly was happy for her, but she still couldn't understand why they'd come all the way to Lubbock. "That's great."

Josiah slipped his hands into his jean's pockets. "Brenda has a few things to tell you, but she wanted to do it in person."

Looking from Brenda to Josiah, Molly asked, "What things?"

"Why don't we sit at that picnic table over there?" Josiah tipped his head toward a covered table a few feet away.

They crossed the short distance and sat down. Josiah and Molly on one side, Brenda on the other. It felt awkward sitting across from her, knowing she was trying to take Ellie away.

Before she could stop herself, Molly blurted, "Why do you want to take Ellie from me?"

"I don't."

Now Molly was truly confused. "Then—"

Brenda smiled. "Your mom called me a couple of weeks ago when Derek got the parental termination rights. He was on the call with her, and they were saying they wanted to take Ellie from you."

"So you weren't part of that?"

"No," she said, shaking her head. "Derek is not Ellie's father. I told your mom that on the phone. I felt bad for lying, but I'd just come out of an abusive relationship, and Derek was nice to me."

Molly felt clubbed over the head. "My brother isn't Ellie's dad?"

"When I found out I was pregnant, I told him it was his. He seemed so happy, but the longer I was with him, the more I realized that neither of us was able to take care of a baby." Brenda paused, fidgeting with her fingers, not quite meeting Molly's gaze. "Then I met you. You didn't judge me or try to force me to do anything. It was the first time anyone had been so kind to me. I wanted you to take Ellie, but I was afraid if you found out Derek wasn't the father, you wouldn't want the baby."

Josiah leaned forward with his arms on the table. "If Derek isn't the father, who is?"

Brenda tucked a piece of hair behind her ear and stared at the table. "His name was Orion Hyde."

"Was?" Molly asked.

"I found out he died of a drug overdose shortly after I left him."

Molly was struggling to keep her thoughts in order. "So, if my mom and brother know Ellie isn't Derek's, why are they threatening to take her?"

Shrugging, Brenda said, "They said they didn't believe me, and I told them to go ahead and have a paternity test done."

Raking her hand through her hair, Molly tried to catch her breath. Ellie wasn't Derek's child. A smile stretched on her lips. "So a single paternity test will prove that?"

Brenda nodded. "His name isn't even on the birth certificate." She pinched her lips together. "He knew that."

"So, he kinda thought Ellie wasn't his from the beginning?" asked Josiah.

"I think so," Brenda replied. "I'm not fighting the termination of rights. I spoke to your lawyer this morning and told her everything. Mostly, I just wanted to talk to you, Molly, and tell you thanks for adopting Ellie."

Tears pooled in Molly's eyes and trickled down her cheeks. "I love her so very much. I can't thank you enough for letting me have her."

Brenda and Molly stood at the same time and embraced. Now they were both crying. "You helped me see my worth, Molly. I'll never be able to repay you."

Josiah's phone rang, and Molly looked at him. Work on New Year's Eve? And right in the middle of this?

He stood, walked a few feet, and put the phone to his ear. Molly didn't care anymore. Whatever he'd paid the lawyer, she'd find a way to pay it back. Her days of being abandoned were over.

She leaned back and smiled at Brenda. "Thank you so much for trusting her with me. I promise to put her first every time, all the time." A promise she could wholeheartedly keep now that she realized Josiah was no different than all the other men in her life.

"I know." Brenda dropped her arms and stepped back. "I need to get back to my family. My grandma is making black-eyed peas and collard greens, and they're the best."

Molly nodded. "Yeah," she said, looking in Josiah's

direction. "We need to get back to Caprock Canyon. His family is waiting on us. Thanks again."

"You too." Brenda turned and walked away.

Josiah approached Molly and smiled. "That was—"

Holding her hand up, Molly stopped him. "It's okay. You don't need to explain. Thank you for bringing me here. I feel like I can breathe again."

"I kinda do need to explain, though. That was Ms. Salinas. She says we should go ahead and get a paternity test. Once it's proven Derek isn't the father, the case is pretty much over. Of course, we'll still have the court appearance, but as soon as the courthouse opens again, she says we'll get the extension so the test can be administered."

Now she felt a tiny bit guilty for automatically assuming it was work. It didn't change her feelings about things, but at least he'd kept his word. "Okay, when and where does that need to happen?"

"She said she'd get it set up after the new year."

Nodding, Molly hugged herself. "Thank you."

Josiah hugged her, and she stiffened. She needed to set things straight. Pulling free, she stepped back. "Josiah, I appreciate everything you've done for me and Ellie, from the teddy bear to the lawyer, but I made a promise to Brenda that I intend to keep."

His eyebrows knitted together. "Okay. What does that mean?"

"It means that the last few weeks have been emotional, and I crossed a line I shouldn't have. I promised her Ellie would be my first priority. You're a great guy, but I made a rule that I wouldn't date while Ellie was young. I mean it, and I'm keeping that promise." Molly could see the pain in his eyes, but she couldn't and wouldn't let herself be swayed. Sooner or later, he'd leave, and she knew it.

"Right. I, uh, I know. It's okay." He smiled the world's saddest smile. It barely lifted the corners of his lips. "We should probably get back so we can watch the fireworks."

Molly took his hand in hers. "I'm not trying to hurt your feelings."

His smile widened. "You didn't. Ellie comes first, and that's the way it should be." He pulled his hand away and hooked a thumb toward the truck. "Let's get on the road."

Turning, she watched him walk toward his pickup. The closer he got, the more rounded his shoulders became. She'd hurt him, and for that, she was deeply sorry. Part of her wanted to run after him, but that was quickly drowned out by the logical part of her brain. The one that said it was better for him to hurt now than later.

This was the right move. But even as she thought it, a small voice chastised her. For the first time in her life, she'd done the walking away, and it felt just as bad as all those times people had walked away from her.

CHAPTER 20

The awkward silence between Josiah and Molly lasted the entire drive back to the ranch. What could he say? He'd known from the very beginning that she didn't want to date. Did it really matter that he'd planned to tell her he loved her and didn't care about a stupid award?

With all the kissing they'd done, he thought she'd changed her mind. He wasn't thinking it was stress or worry drawing them closer, but he should have realized it before letting his heart run wild. Now he not only didn't care about the award, but he didn't have Molly and Ellie either. Hurt didn't begin to cover how he felt.

While everyone else was outside watching fireworks, he brought Ellie inside. The loud noises scared her, and he wasn't in a festive mood. As he cradled her in his arms, he slowly packed his suitcase. They wouldn't be leaving until January 2nd, but this way he'd have a head start on it.

He was so torn between wanting to make their stay last as long as possible and wanting time to speed up so he could get it over with. Molly hadn't said it in so many words, but when they got back to Dallas, she wouldn't be working for him anymore. Not only was he losing her, but he was pretty sure he was losing Ellie too.

"Josiah," his mom called his name as she entered his room. "If you want, I can watch Ellie while you enjoy the fireworks."

He turned, and her gaze landed on his half-full suitcase. "You're already packing?"

"Yeah, Molly said she wants to get back to Dallas so she's available for the lawyer." It wasn't a total lie, but it wasn't the absolute truth either.

She closed the distance between them. "Are you okay?"

Nodding, he handed Ellie to her. "Yeah, I'm fine."

"You're really a terrible liar. You know that, right?" She set her hand on his upper arm and rubbed it. "Now, what's wrong?"

"I let myself get a little too carried away with

Molly. She doesn't want a relationship, and I knew that. I should have kept my distance, and I didn't. I'll be fine." He went to move, but his mom stopped him.

She took her hand from his arm and clasped his hand, squeezing it. "It's been a rough few weeks for her. I can't begin to understand what she's been going through. Maybe give her a little time to sort herself out. I know she cares about you."

"Maybe," he said softly. "Did Dad tell you I'm thinking of moving back?"

"He did, and I can't say I wasn't tickled pink. Is that what you want to do?" She shifted Ellie to her shoulder, and Ellie belched. "My goodness." She leaned back and looked down at the baby. "You feel better, huh?"

Laughing, Josiah checked his mom's shoulder for spit-up. "Wow, nothing. Just air, I guess."

"Her poor tummy was hurting, I bet. She's such an easy baby." His mom patted Ellie's bottom. "These are the kind of babies that lull women into wanting more. Then they have a few more and they get a Wyatt West—who made up for all of you in one shot."

"I remember. I thought he'd never stop trying to kick me in the face."

"Me either." She smiled. "So, back to you moving. Are you sure you want to do that?"

He sat on the edge of his bed next to his suitcase.

"Yeah, I think so. As the ranch grows, so will the town. Bear isn't finished hiring people. They'll need grocery stores, schools, and all the other things that come with having a town. It's actually a great time to move back."

There was also a rumor floating that oil was found between Caprock and Amarillo. If that was the case, it wouldn't just be Bear's employees needing homes; it would be oil-field workers too.

"Well, you won't have me talking you out of it. I'd love to have all my kids close again."

"I've missed being home too." He paused. "Case has wanted my apartment since I bought it." Neither of them knew it at the time, but they'd been bidding against each other. A year later, Case was looking for another place to rent when he contacted Josiah through a referral. For a second, it had been a little weird, but there were no hard feelings. From there, they'd become great friends.

His mom walked to the door. "Go outside and enjoy the fireworks. I think we're going to play a card game while we watch the ball drop."

Standing, Josiah sighed and followed her out of the room. He didn't feel like watching fireworks, but he wasn't going to argue with his mom. Maybe they'd lift his spirits. Probably not. At this point, his spirits felt buried, and he didn't have the energy to dig them out.

He was pretty certain it would be a while before they left the ground again.

His mom waved as she stepped into her room, and he continued down the stairs, grabbing his coat before stepping outside. He draped it over his arm and sat down in the closest rocker. It was cold, but the crisp air felt good against his skin.

In the distance, he could see Molly talking to Carrie Anne, Reagan, and Gabby. A few feet away, Wyatt stood with Hunter while their dad held Tucker and pointed to the sky.

This was almost how he'd pictured the day ending. Instead of sitting on the porch, he would be standing next to Molly with his arm around her, starting the new year with her beside him. He was going to tell her he loved her and didn't care about Realtor of the Year or any of that. He was choosing her and Ellie.

Moving back home was a wise choice. It would give him the opportunity to be near family and the distance he'd need to get over Molly. He'd never stop loving Ellie, but eventually, maybe he could move on enough that he could find someone to share his life with. At least, that was his hope.

Looking over her shoulder, Molly spied Josiah sitting in a rocking chair. His mom let her know she was going to watch Ellie so he could see a few of the fireworks.

He'd been abnormally quiet the whole ride home from Lubbock. She really hadn't meant to hurt him, but she wasn't giving in this time. No matter how hurt and dejected he seemed, she knew she'd made the right choice, both for her and Ellie but also for him. He could focus on his career, and she could focus on raising Ellie.

Reagan nudged Molly's arm. "You can go talk to him. I'm positive he won't bite."

Molly pulled her gaze from Josiah back to Reagan. "I'm okay."

"Right."

"I am." Molly could hear the indecision in her voice. "I really am okay. This is for the best."

Reagan took her hand and pulled her away from the group. Once they were out of earshot, she stopped. "Last year at this time, I was so angry I could have spit nails. I thought Hunter had betrayed me. It was the worst feeling in the world."

"But that was a different situation." Plus, Reagan didn't know what it was like to have people letting her down all the time.

"Not really. He's stolen your heart, and once you decide to let someone hold your world in their hands, heartache always follows."

Molly crossed her arms over her chest. "If this is your idea of a pep talk, you should stick with coffee."

Chuckling, Reagan shook her head. "People are people. They will inevitably let you down because they're human. No one is perfect. Are you saying you won't ever hurt Josiah? Because by the looks of him, you already have. It's part of trusting someone. If there is one thing this family has taught me, you never quit trying."

"I'm not quitting. We want different things." Molly dropped her arms to her sides. "I've made my mind up, and I'm not changing it. I appreciate what you're trying to do, but I've got Ellie, and she's all I need."

Reagan gathered Molly into a hug. "Okay." After a hard squeeze, Reagan leaned back. "You have my number. If you ever need anything, you give me a call."

Molly had everyone's phone number, and they'd all said the same thing. She thought it was really kind of them. Not that she planned on taking them up on it, but the gesture was wonderful. "Thank you."

"You're family. You won't ever not be family. Not to me, and definitely not to the Wests and Fredericks."

Nodding, Molly smiled. "I know. They're really great people."

"Incredible is more like it. My parents already had plans this year, or they would have been here. So would my sister, Carlin. I think Carrie Anne is salivating to get her here just so she can fix her up with someone."

They both laughed. "You think she'll ever open up a matchmaking service?"

"Seriously? Yes. The girl is actually really good at it." They both looked in Carrie Anne's direction. "She's going to be an amazing mom. I don't think the girl has a mean bone in her body. Israel says she wasn't always like this, but it's hard to picture her any other way."

Molly's gaze drifted to the porch where she'd last seen Josiah. The chair was empty, and when she searched the crowd, he wasn't with them either. Inwardly, she grumbled. Reagan was wrong on this one. Josiah and Molly weren't meant to be, and despite the tiny voice she continued to tamp down, she wasn't having a change of heart.

Ellie deserved a life free of the kind of pain Molly endured, and Molly's renewed determination would see to it that Ellie's life was as close to perfect as it could get.

CHAPTER 21

After returning to Dallas, Josiah had dropped Molly and Ellie off at their apartment. He'd offered to watch Ellie from time to time, but he'd gotten the distinct impression that he wouldn't be seeing either of them for a while, if ever.

It had been a painfully long drive from the ranch, and he'd felt broken as he drove off from her apartment, leaving the two people he loved most in the world. In a bid to take his mind off of it, he'd invited Case over to talk about the apartment. If Josiah was moving, he wanted to get it done. The more distance between him and Dallas, the better.

The doorbell rang, and Josiah jogged to the door and pulled it open. "Hey, Case."

"Hey," his friend said and shook his hand, stepping

inside. "There are times when I think you invite me here to rub it in that you won it."

With a laugh, Josiah walked to the kitchen and pulled out a few bottles of Dr. Pepper, the state beverage of Texas. "Actually, that's why you're here."

"So you admit it!" He laughed as he took the offered drink.

"No, I'm saying if you want it, it's yours. I want to move back home."

Case stared a Josiah a moment. "What?"

"I'm moving back home. Do you want the apartment or not?" Josiah asked and took a long drag of his drink.

"Yeah, I want it. Why are you moving, though?" Case followed Josiah to the couch and sat in the adjacent chair.

Josiah shrugged. "I miss my family. Plus, there's a good opportunity there to sell real estate now that the town is coming back to life."

His friend eyed him, and one lone eyebrow arched up. "And the girl has nothing to do with it?"

"She does, but I was going to move home either way." Not totally true, but close enough.

"Did Diane help you guys?"

"Yeah, she was awesome. She suggested we talk to the birth mom, and we did. I can't say much because

It's not my story to tell, but I think things are going to be okay."

Sitting back, Case set his ankle over his knee. "Good to know. Diane is tough. She makes me glad I went into entertainment law."

"That reminds me. I sent Malakai some properties, and he liked one of them, but I'm guessing you already know that since you're his lawyer."

"Yeah, he called. On New Year's Day. Does the guy not understand holidays?"

"I don't think so, but I think it's because he's never been told no. That's what happens when you grow up as a Dallas socialite." Josiah paused. "He's a decent guy, though. He helped me get a great detective. That's how we were able to find the birth mom so quickly."

Case nodded. "He is a good guy when you get to know him. The first time I met him, I wanted to punch him."

Laughing, Josiah added, "You too?"

"So, this moving thing. You're really serious? Because if you are, I want the apartment."

"Can you get out of your current lease?"

"Yeah, totally. It'll cost me, but that's okay. I've only got a few months left on the one I'm in currently." He finished off his drink and set the bottle next to the chair. "I've got some free time. I drove by that old theater on the way here. They're playing *Goonies*. You want to go see it?"

Josiah's heart ached. Molly would want to see that. "Uh, how about that new movie with the zombies?"

Case sat forward. "Oh, man, she got you good if you're turning down a classic."

"It's okay. I just need a little time."

Grabbing the bottle, Case stood. "Okay. Let's go watch zombies eat brains."

"Thanks," Josiah said and pushed off the couch. "And thanks for coming over."

"No problem, man. Heartbreak is a bear."

Sugar-free gummy bears. And now he had no one willing to fight them off. Hopefully, it wouldn't take long to get over Molly or everything he loved reminding him of her. The dull ache in his chest grew a little bigger, and he had a feeling it would be a while. His problem was that he didn't really want to get over her. How could you force yourself to stop loving someone? He wasn't sure anyone would have the answer to that.

CHAPTER 22

It had been a month since Josiah dropped Molly off at her apartment. The second his taillights disappeared around the corner, she'd dissolved into a mess of tears. She'd made a decision, and her heart wasn't on board at all. Still, even with all the waterworks, she'd convinced herself that she was just being emotional and needed to stick to her rule.

With each day that passed, she doubted herself more and more. Josiah was a good man with a beautiful heart. He'd given her a job when he didn't have to. He'd invited her home. He'd changed a diaper that most men would have run from. Reagan's words continued to ring in her ears. Love was a risk. The real question Molly had to ask herself was, was it a risk she was willing to take? What if she got hurt again?

The question was always answered with another question. What if she didn't? Her heart and her head were giving her whiplash. She'd walked past the old theater and saw that *Goonies* was playing. Then "Tainted Love" came on the intercom while she was applying for a job. She'd started bawling and left because she couldn't see through the tears to fill it out.

"Molly." The sound of Ms. Salinas's voice cut through her thoughts as Molly sat in the lobby of her office.

She swallowed down the tears currently threatening to spill and lifted her head. "Hi."

Ms. Salinas was smiling at her. "Come on in."

Two days ago, she'd taken Ellie for the paternity test, and the results were back. As much as she wanted to believe Brenda, part of her couldn't stop worrying until that test backed up her claim. What if Brenda didn't really know if Ellie was Derek's or not? Derek stayed with her, so he must have thought there was a chance the baby was his, right?

"Thanks, Ms. Salinas." Molly stood. Normally she would have brought Ellie with her, but it had been pouring for a week. Instead, Molly had left her with the babysitter.

The lawyer looked from Molly to another woman

sitting in the lobby. A woman Molly hadn't noticed before. "Emilia Sanger?"

"That's me," the woman said and stood.

Who was she, and why was Molly's attorney asking her into the office at the same time as Molly? She obviously wasn't hiding her confusion as she followed Emilia into Ms. Salinas's office.

The woman turned as the door shut and stuck her hand out. "I'm the private detective Josiah West hired to find Brenda. My friend Malakai Raven recommended me."

"The lead singer of Crush?"

Talk about a piece of work. The guy was known for throwing tantrums when he didn't get his way. It wasn't even a week ago that a news story popped up on Molly's Twitter feed that he'd ticked off the entire population of France.

"That's the one. The guy is a pest sometimes, but he's got a good heart." Emilia took a seat in one of the chairs opposite the attorney. "It's getting past that throat-punchable exterior that's a real beast." She laughed.

"So, Josiah hired you…"

"Shortly after Christmas," Emilia answered.

Shortly after…Christmas. The call she thought was business. Josiah was hiring a private detective? Oh, no.

He'd been doing something for her, and she'd thrown it back in his face because she was…a coward.

Ms. Salina nodded. "Yeah, Josiah left me a message when he hired her. It was a good thing he did, too. Finding out your brother wasn't the biological father pretty much closed the case. Which brings me to why we're here."

Right. Why Molly was there. Either the battle was over or it was just beginning. "Right."

"Derek is not Ellie's father. Brenda was telling the truth. The man who fathered her passed from a drug overdose." Ms. Salinas nodded to Emilia. "Thanks to Emilia's quick work, we have that verified as well."

Molly let out the breath she'd been holding and wilted. No more fighting. And as great as the news was, Josiah should have been there to hear it. If it weren't for Molly, he *would* have been there.

She'd been stupid. Reagan was right. She'd been terrified of being hurt, and she'd used anything she could hold on to, to justify running away.

After this meeting, she'd find him. Hopefully, he'd let her apologize and smother him in kisses after she begged him to forgive her.

Ms. Salinas continued. "After presenting the information to your mother's attorney, they have decided to drop the custody challenge."

"Thank you so much," Molly said and stood. "I probably should go find Josiah and tell him the good news."

Ms. Salinas's eyebrows furrowed. "Uh, he moved. I thought you'd know that."

"Moved?"

She nodded. "Back to his hometown. I think maybe a week ago. He'd intended to be here today, but he left a message overnight that he wouldn't be able to make it. He has a cold and didn't want to pass it along to the baby."

"Okay. Uh, thank you for letting me know."

"Is everything okay?" Emilia asked.

Molly smiled. "Everything's fine." Well, it wasn't, but she was sending a thousand prayers up that everything *would* be fine. She wasn't sure how she was going to fix things, but she was desperate for Josiah.

Risks sometimes hurt, and she was willing to have her heart shattered into a million little pieces if there was even a tiny sliver of hope that he'd give her a second chance.

She'd hold his precious heart with the softest hands and guard it as fiercely as she knew how. It was time to call in that offer Reagan made.

CHAPTER 23

After a long day of emptying a moving truck filled with furniture, the last thing Josiah wanted to do was drive to the ranch. He'd tried hard to get out of it, but his dad had insisted he needed the kind of help only Josiah could give. Finally, he'd relented and promised he'd be there as quickly as he could.

Parking his pickup in front of the house, he cut the engine and stepped outside. He took the steps at a jog and froze as the door opened.

"Molly?"

"It's freezing. Where is your coat?" she asked.

"I was hot." He blinked a few times. "What are you doing here?"

She took him by the hand and pulled him into the house. "I need to talk to you."

He softly shut the door and stayed by it. "Talk to me about what? And where is all my family? Where is Ellie?"

"Ellie's with your mom. She's not Derek's, by the way."

"Brenda said she wasn't."

"I have trust issues." She paused. "Your family went to the orchard so I could talk to you alone."

His eyebrows knitted together. "Okay."

Molly held his gaze a moment longer and then began pacing. "I royally messed up, Josiah. So many times, people walked out on me, and I didn't want it happening again. I wanted to be the one to walk out on someone before they hurt me, so I did. And you know what?" She stopped pacing and faced him. "It hurt worse."

"What?"

Groaning, she palmed her forehead. "I thought that call after Christmas was you choosing work over me and Ellie. I was a jerk because I took one little thing and used it against you. Even if it was work, when you did give me and Ellie your attention, we had all of it. Nothing and no one is perfect, but that's the standard I was using."

He didn't know how to process what he was hearing. "But your rule."

"The stupidest rule ever made. This whole last month, I've been a complete mess. I can't watch *Goonies*. No one ever calls me. Not one single person, but then Ms. Salinas calls, and my phone starts ringing. I lost it. It's the *Sharknado* theme song, and I'm in the middle of the grocery store, crying like I'd lost my best friend…" She took a few steps toward him. "Because I had."

"You cried over *Sharknado*?" he asked, closing a little of the gap between them.

Closing the remaining distance, she nodded. "I'm so sorry I hurt you. I will never be able to say it enough. Do you think you can ever forgive me? I'd rather be Sam to your Danny Phantom than anyone else on earth. I don't want to sing "Tainted Love" ever again without your cat-dying notes destroying the chorus."

"Cat-dying notes?"

She shrugged. "I kinda overheard you singing to Ellie, so it's just a guess. I love you, Josiah. I was so worried about getting hurt that I didn't realize it would hurt worse to not love you."

Chuckling, he smiled. "I love you too. I don't want anything but you and Ellie. Loving you, loving Ellie, that's all the success I need. Without the two of you, success means nothing to me."

"Does that mean you forgive me for being a complete and total jerk?"

"I think that's pretty much the definition of a relationship: messing up and apologizing over and over until we grow old and gray." He wrapped his arms around her and pulled her to him. "I'd like that very much."

She lifted on her toes as she circled her arms around his neck. "Me too."

The last word was barely out of her mouth before she kissed him. It was like the last puzzle piece snapping into place, making the picture whole. Molly, Ellie, and him. They were three pieces who fit together perfectly. They were worth so much more than an award.

His arms tightened around her as he deepened the kiss, and it felt like he'd been brought back to life. The past month, he'd ached in ways he'd never thought possible, and now, he was holding the one dream he wanted most in the world. A home with the two people he loved most.

Slowly, the kiss came to an end, and he leaned back. "So, about that marriage—"

"Yes."

"Usually, the girl lets the guy finish." He grinned.

"Yeah, but I think we've established I'm not like other girls." She laughed.

He kissed her nose. "I love it. I love you."

"I love you."

"Let's go get Ellie. I've missed her." He stepped back and took Molly's hand. Walking through life with her would be fun.

EPILOGUE

Three months later...

Molly smiled as she held Josiah's gaze.

"I, Josiah, take you, Molly, to be my partner in life. I'd sing, but I think we've learned that's not something I should do outside of the shower."

Their friends and family laughed along with Molly and Josiah. It had been three long months for her, waiting to pledge her heart to him. They'd decided to marry once Ellie's adoption was finalized. Josiah had already started the process to add West to her last name.

Josiah continued. "I choose you. I love that you read comics, that we can have conversations with music lyrics, and I love how you love our little girl. I'd say you're the best mom ever, but I don't want to get into a fight. I bruise easily."

Again, everyone laughed. He always had a knack for making her laugh. One of the things she loved most of all about him.

His laughter died, and their eyes locked. "I choose you, and because I choose you, this I promise: I will always hold your heart with care. I will always walk toward you, not away. I will always be present for you and Ellie. I will share my Milk Duds and not steal your Nerds. Most of all, I promise to love you with my whole heart for as long as I have breath."

She flung her arms around his neck and kissed him. The small group laughed again.

"Uh, that's at the end," the minister said.

Molly stepped back and wiped her eyes. "Sorry. I've found that I have an excellent knack for breaking rules." She grew serious as she looked at Josiah. "For all the right reasons."

"You can say your vows now, Molly," the minister said.

Glancing at their family and friends, she caught her mom's gaze and smiled. Her mom and stepdad were attending the wedding. He'd even given Molly away.

It had taken a few meetings and a lot of tears, but they'd worked out of their issues. Her mom had apologized for trying to take Ellie, and Molly had accepted it. It had gone a long way to healing their relationship. It wasn't completely mended, but Molly could see it heading that way.

She tangled her fingers in Josiah's, holding his gaze. "I, Molly, choose you, Josiah, for as long as I have breath. You're the person I want to hold and be held by. You're the person I want to love and be loved by. I love how you love Ellie. I love how you give so selflessly. I cherish your heart, your soul, and your mind. I love the person you are and that you hold my heart. There's no one else on earth I'd rather walk beside than you."

The minister led them through exchanging their rings and then presented them to the group. "I now pronounce you husband and wife. You may kiss the bride."

Josiah took her face in his hands and kissed her as everyone cheered. The best day was finalizing Ellie's adoption, and her wedding to Josiah was tied with it.

Never in her life would she have thought that getting fired from that coffee shop would be the best thing to ever happen to her, but it was. If there was one thing that she'd learned through this whole experience, it was that good things could come from the bad.

For a list of all books by Bree Livingston, please visit her website at www.breelivingston.com.

ABOUT THE AUTHOR

Bree Livingston lives in the West Texas Panhandle with her husband, children, and cats. She'd have a dog, but they took a vote and the cats won. Not in numbers, but attitude. They wouldn't even debate. They just leveled their little beady eyes at her and that was all it took for her to nix getting a dog. Her hobbies include...nothing because she writes all the time.

She loves carbs, but the love ends there. No, that's not true. The love usually winds up on her hips which is why she loves writing romance. The love in the pages of her books are sweet and clean, and they definitely don't add pounds when you step on the scale. Unless of course, you're actually holding a Kindle while you're weighing. Put the Kindle down and try again. Also, the cookie because that could be the problem too. She knows from experience.

Join her mailing list to be the first to find out

publishing news, contests, and more by going to her website at https://www.breelivingston.com.

- facebook.com/BreeLivingstonWrites
- twitter.com/BreeLivWrites
- bookbub.com/authors/bree-livingston

Printed in Great Britain
by Amazon